Ghost Train

D1528613

Copyright © 2019 by Dave Brown

All rights reserved.

Cover and book design by Jeremy Brown, unlocklayer.com

*No part of this book may be reproduced in any form or by
any electronic or mechanical means including information
storage and retrieval systems, without permission in
writing from the author. The only exception is by a
reviewer, who may quote short excerpts in a review.*

*This book is a work of fiction. Names, characters, places, and
incidents are either products of the author's imagination
or are used fictiously. Any resemblance to actual persons,
living or dead, events or locales is entirely coincidental.*

Visit our website at ghosttrainbook.com

First Printing: June 2019
ISBN: 978-10-70158-04-4

This book is dedicated to my wife, who retrieved it out of a box in the closet, dusted it off, after fourteen years or more, being "left for dead" and kicked me in the butt to finish it.

And to my son Jeremy, who has spent multiple hours of his time teaching me how to use an iPad, editing all of my mistakes, structuring it, building a website, working to get it published and many other high-tech thing that I don't understand.

And to God, who gave me the many recurring dreams and nightmares over the past twenty-six years that created the foundation for this story and many others.

THE BEGINNING OF THE END

The September air was clean and brisk. The morning sun made its slow journey over the pristine mountain tops. It had been raining all night long and barely stopped an hour ago. The early morning sun was burning off the remaining wispy fog, and an exhilarating mist was lingering on the aging, steel framing, of the Kurtzville, railroad trestle. Droplets of dew bounced off his head and arms, making things a little slippery for Jack Beckman. He took a deep breath, filling his lungs with the sweet morning air and the fragrance of wild flowers. He adjusted his headphones and cranked up his favorite tune, *Don't Fear The Reaper.*

He was hanging 165 feet in the air, on a newly purchased, ¾" nylon rope, that was attached to his pick-up truck, above and the other end, was secured to his safety harness. He felt like a well-seasoned construction worker, that was swinging high from an I-beam, on a New York City skyscraper…damn he felt good…

He had a job to do, for which he was being very well compensated to complete. He was hired a few weeks ago by some guy that he met in his neighborhood bar, *The Last Chance.* It got its name because it was the last bar going out of town. Most of the "good old boys" hung out there for two reasons, one, because their pick-up trucks wouldn't be spotted there by wives or family, and secondly, the cops never venture out there, unless there was a bar room fight. It was a "good watering hole" as the boys put it, and it had a vintage jukebox, over in a dusty corner, that played all 70's tunes, which pleased Jack, to know end.

His new-found friend, that hired him, instructed Jack to place several packages under the old train trestle, and carefully install them in certain locations, indicated on a makeshift map, that he had previously given to him. Now Jack was by no means, a genius, but he had a good idea what the contents of each package held, but at this point, in his lousy life, he didn't much give a rat's ass, what was in them. The amount of money that he was making from this meager job, would pay off his all his credit cards, his used car payments and even put a considerable amount away for college, for his eight year old daughter. Jack carefully worked, planting the 'packages', at their designated locations. He adjusted his earbuds, cranked up his tune's, and sang along

> *La…La…la…la, la*
> *Don't fear the reaper,*
> *Baby I'm your man…*
> *La…la…la…la la*
> *Romeo and Juliet…*
> *Are together in eternity*

Moving from one steel beam to another, he thought about

the vacation that he and his family never took. His wife pestered him all the time to take her and Amy, his daughter, to Disney World, but they never could afford it. Between high gas prices, skyrocketing health insurance, and low salaries, they were lucky to make ends meet...

Jack had stopped for a quick one on a Friday night, after work, two or three weeks ago. When he walked into the bar, the smelled the stale cigarette smoke instantly hit him, and the front door made its old familiar squeaking sound, like someone was pulling a nail out of well-seasoned oak. He turned to Luke, the bartender, and asked him when he was going to get his skinny ass over here, and oil the hinges. That brought some laughs from the regulars. He walked over to the well, worn bar, and settled down on his stool, just as Luke was handing him an ice-cold mug of Bud. It was a warm night for September and he had a mighty thirst, he lifted his mug and chugged it.

"That's on me," an out-of-Towner stated. Jack glanced over and said thanks, as he sat the mug down, trying to put a name to the face. But he had never seen this guy before. He was a very large man, maybe six five or more, and at least three hundred pounds. He was well dressed and clean shaven, he looked like one of the characters from the show, *The Soprano's* Jack instantly became apprehensive, and wondered if he owed somebody money, big money. That thought stayed with him, as he continued drinking. He ended up getting buzzed and shooting two or three games of pool with his new friend, who seemed to be the nicest guy he had ever met. After talking with him for an hour or two, Jack felt that he knew him, as good as he knew his own brother. The guy bought drinks all night long for Jack. After a while, he got down to business and discussed a small job, then asked Jack if he was interested. He told Jack that it would be a good deal for him, and after all, Jack could never turn down a good deal...

THE DEAL

Jack and his new-found friend, Dave, talked into the wee hours of the morning. He was convinced that this deal was right for him. At first, he felt like he was selling his soul to the devil, but that feeling quickly faded away when Dave discreetly, handed him an envelope full of hundreds.

"This is just a little down payment Jack" Dave whispered. "You'll get the big payoff after you complete your assignment." He was grinning at Jack as he handed him the money, his eyes were as dark as coal. Jack was hesitant as he accepted the money from Dave's big hands. He had a bad feeling in his gut…but the thickness of the envelope, quickly took that feeling away.

Jack headed for home, eager to count his money. It was after 1 A.M. when he crept into his home. He slowly opened the kitchen screen door, being super careful not to wake anyone up. Then he unlocked the deadbolt on the wood door and crossed the room and sat down at the old porcelain, kitchen table. The aroma of a well-cooked pot roast, still filled the air…"*shit….*"He thought, *"he missed dinner again…"* He slowly opened the envelope and counted his money…"*…five grand.*" He whispered out loud, he wanted to scream out with joy, but that would wake up Alice and Amy, and cause all sorts of problems. He couldn't believe his good luck, *"what a piece of cake, and this is just the down payment"* he thought to himself…

THE DEED

So here he was, two weeks later, swinging on his new rope, pulling packs of C-4, out of his gunnysack, and placing *"little surprise packages"* here and there, like a reverse, Easter-egg hunt…He had no idea what he was doing, but his new friend

Dave, had given him simple instructions and explained that it was as easy as 1,2,3, and, so far it was. Jack was thinking this was pretty cool, as he moved up another few feet on the train trestle and placed another package. He took a big breath of fresh morning air, slowly exhaled and started reminiscing about his life. He was never good at sports, he always got into trouble trying to be the "tough guy", but that was hard to do when you were the smallest guy in class. Girls didn't pay much attention to him, let alone date him. The guys would teased him and never picked him to play on their teams, they called him "runt." But now, *he* was the king of the mountain...

After placing a total of twenty-one packages, he reached the top of the trestle, looked at his watched.

"9:15, not bad" he mused, "one lousy hour of work, shit man, I'm rich!"

He was smiling from ear to ear as he began packing up his gear. His mission was completed. He stuffed all his new gear into an army surplus, canvas bag, stowed it in the back of his pick-up and headed for home.

At a red light he pulled out the cell phone,that Dave had given him. As per instructions, he tapped the only listed number and Dave answered instantly.

"Jack" he stated, with self-assurance, "I assumed everything went as planned?"

"You bet it did." Jack answered proudly.

"Good Jack, very good."There was a slight pause on Dave's end. Jack tensed up. He had a bad feeling about this whole deal, and thought Dave was going to screw him over.

"Now Jack, I've already wired the money to your bank account, so you and your family are rich. But Jack," again a slight pause. Jack started to panic. "there's one more thing you have to do for me, okay, pal?"

"What's that, sir?" Jack asked, nervously...

"Now Jack, don't call me sir. We're buddies, remember?"

Another pause, Jack was starting to sweat.

"Now listen very carefully Jack…using the cellphone I gave you, you know, the one you're using right now Jack…call the number that I'm going to give you, at exactly 10:19 a.m.., and Jack, make sure it is exactly 10:19 a.m.., understand Jack?" Dave's voice was very stern at this point.

"I've got it Sir, aah, I mean Dave…Sir, aah…" Jack studdered, his hands were shaking, "ah, what's the number Dave?"

"Okay Jack, do you have a pen?"

"Ah, wait a second, I'm going to pull off the road so I can punch the number into the phone…Alright, I'm ready, go ahead…"

"Five-five-five, one-two, one-two. Got it Jack? Five-five-five, one-two, one-two."

"Yes Sir, no problem, five-five-five, one-two, one-two. At exactly 10:19 a.m. I got it."

"Oh, and Jack, when you're finished making the phone call…destroy the phone. Smash it with a hammer, stomp on it, burn it, whatever you want, just make sure it's destroyed, then toss it into the river, you got it Jack? Good bye Jack."

The phone went dead before Jack could answer. His hands were shaking as he lay the cell phone on his seat. His stomach was turning. His head was pounding. He definitely needed a drink. So instead of going home he made a detour straight to the Last Chance.

He kicked up dust as he pulled into the dirt parking lot. As he shut off the engine, he glanced into the rear-view mirror to see if anyone was following him. He had a nervous feeling in his gut again, but blew the feeling off just thinking about all that money. He got out of his pick-up and looked all around, everything looked normal. The Yuengling beer sign, in the window, was tilted to the left, as usual. The juke box was playing a Johnny Cash tune, and the back door was propped open for the beer delivery guy.

"Yep…everything's normal" Jack confirmed out loud, the door squeaked as he walked in, three guys were sitting at the bar, and a local girl was dropping a quarter into the jukebox. He ordered a double shot and a frosted mug of Bud.

"Little early to be drinking like that, ain't it Jack?" Luke asked.

"Naw," Jack replied, "I got up early this morning and did some fishing, now I just want to kick back and relax."

"Sounds good my man. Want anything to eat?"

"Nope, just give me a round, I might have a bite later." Luke tipped the bottle of Seagram's and poured him a double, then he grabbed a mug out of the freezer and poured him a fresh Bud. He took Jack's money, and rang it up, in the old brass register, then he headed down to the other end of the bar and waited on a customer and started a conversation with him. Jack looked at his watch:

10:00 a.m.

Almost time for the call.

He downed the shot and finished off his mug of bud, and asked for another round. Then he reached into his shirt pocket, pulled out his Marlboro's, tapped the pack on the bar top, lit one up, and took a big drag and finally started to relaxed. His mind started to wander, thinking of how great the vacation was going to be…

He got up and walked to the men's room. He carefully checked it out to make sure he was alone, then he opened the stall door and sat down on the commode. As instructed, at exactly 10:19 a.m., he made the phone call. It rang several times. No answer. He waited for a few more rings, then hung up.

"What the hell," he whispered to himself, "did I fuck up that number? I know he said five-five-five, one-two, one-two, right?" He tried the number again…complete silence…nothing at all this time…He sat there and thought it over for a couple of minutes…then he took a slow walk back to the bar and ordered another shot and beer, wondering if he should destroy the phone or wait for somebody to call back, and tell him that he fucked up. The girl playing the jukebox, asked him if he wanted to dance. He turned her down.

After a few more beers and a good buzz, he decided to head home. He slightly stumbled when he got off of the bar stool.

"You all right Jack?" Luke yelled over.

"Yeah…I'm fine, just some mud on the bottom of my boots…made me slip is all…I'm going to head home now, see you guys later."

He tried not to stagger, but it was very difficult and his empty stomach churned as he walked out the door. He walked over to his pick-up and fumbled with his keys. He knew he was too drunk to drive, but he didn't dare call for a ride.

He finally made it home, got out of the truck and headed towards the house, he stopped, turned around and walked back to the truck, opened up the door. He pulled the cell phone out of the pocket of his dirty jean jacket, shut it off and threw it under the seat. He would smash it later, right now all he wanted to do was sleep. He quietly closed the door and headed for the house. He sat down on the front porch and removed his boots. Then he tip-toed over to the front door and tried to insert his key into the lock. It hit the floor instead. He struggled to pick it up. Swearing under his breath, he reached down and carefully reclaimed it. Finally, he gained entrance on the third try. He crept across the carpet and laid down on the couch, he hit the remote control and fell asleep instantly…

He didn't see the news bulletin that came on just minutes later, nor did he realize the phone call that he had made, precisely at 10:19 a.m., triggered all 21 packages of plastic dynamite simultaneously, shearing the train trestle into thousands of jagged pieces, creating one of the worst train accidents in railroad history.

The Silver Streak Train approached the trestle at a speed of 240 mph. The world lit up in front of it! It had no chance to slow down, let alone stop. It was engulfed in a mid-air firestorm. Then it plunged to a raging, fiery death, to the bottom of a 190 foot ravine. Explosions and fire were everywhere, trapping all of the 130 passengers, and 12 crew members, in a blazing, twisted, molten steel coffin, suffocating and burning the passengers to death!…

Jack was dreaming about Disney World again and how much fun he and his wife Alice, along with their eight year-old daughter Amy, would have going on the rides, watching the parades and having breakfast with Mickey and Minnie, walking, laughing, shopping, and not having to worry about money. It was going to be perfect.

Jack woke up several hours later. The TV was still on and the breaking news was still about the train wreck. He was instantly glued to the story. He was horrified, because he knew it was him that had created this tragedy.

"Holy shit, ah fuck…shit, what did I do! All that money is never gonna make this feeling go away." And the news story kept repeating:

> …at 10:20 a.m. this morning, a terrorist blew up the Kurtzville train trestle, just east of Pittsburgh, Pa. State Police, FBI, local police and multiple fire/rescue companies are on the scene.

Jack was going out of his mind!
"Alice!," he yelled out, "Alice! Amy! Are you guys upstairs?"

No answer. He jumped off of the couch, and ran up the stairs, scaling them two steps at a time. He tripped on the top stair and tumbled forward, hitting his head and shoulder into the plaster wall. That stunned him for a few seconds, he picked himself up and yelled again. He entered the empty master bedroom, starting to panic. His neck was throbbing and his eye's were watering. Next he tried Amy's room. Nothing looked out of place, bed was made, toys put away…all normal. The only room left upstairs was the bathroom…he knew it was a long shot, but he opened the door and looked in…nothing…

He ran back down the stairs, screaming their names out, as loudly as he could. He turned and ran into the kitchen, his head was still groggy, and on top of it all, he had a horrible hangover. He ran over to the back door and opened it wide open.

"Girls!" he yelled out.

He turned back into the kitchen. "Maybe they went shopping," he thought. That's when he spotted a note on the fridge… He ran over and read it…

Jack, my mother called early this morning said she was very sick and needed me to help her for a few days. So Amy and I are taking the train to help her, see you in a few days…
Love
Alice…xoxoxo
PS: I tried to call you, but you didn't answer…

Jack screamed in horror! "Noooooo! It can't be! There must be some mistake! OH GOD, what have I done!" Jack was in shock, his head hurt so bad, that it felt like a thousand hornets stinging him at the same time. He went to the kitchen sink, bent down, opened the cabinet door and pulled out a bottle of whiskey. He unscrewed the top off and chugged half of the bottle. Then he sat down at the kitchen table, blubbering like a baby as he finished off the whiskey…

He continued sobbing hysterically, pounding his fist on the table, cracking the porcelain. The whiskey bottle shattered, cutting his left hand. He didn't feel any pain.

He stood up and staggered out to his pick-up truck, opened up the passenger door, reached into the glove box, and sat down on the running board. The last sound he ever heard was the blast from his Smith & Wesson.

CHAPTER 1

THE BEGINNING

Dan Jensen looked down at his old Timex watch as he stepped off the subway. He was running ahead of schedule and he enjoyed being on time. That's the way he was raised. As he walked up the subway tunnel stairs, he felt an eerie tingle creep up the back of his neck. It was a strange feeling, like somebody was watching him. He quickly stopped, turned to his right and glanced over his broad shoulder, hoping to see someone or something that would justify this feeling. He tried to shake it off. Nothing was out of place, nobody lurking around the corner, no spies (like you see in the movies). Still, he could still sense something. This feeling, started three or four days ago, right after he purchased his train ticket on line. He probably was just nervous about the trip that he was about to take. He wasn't big on taking long trips, he liked to stay home whenever he could. But since he was going, he got himself all spruced up, for this special occasion, new clothes, haircut, new shoes, even a new hat...

He continued climbing the stairs. When he reached sidewalk level, the bright sunlight hit him square in the eyes. He quickly raised his hand to the brim of his hat to block the blinding rays and in the same instant he stumbled on a raised edge of a concrete pad. He barely caught his balance and looked around to see if anyone had noticed his embarrassing mishap. Loud busses and the city noise, immediately caught his attention. He was breathing a little heavy now and thought he should really lose some weight. His 250 (or more) pounds that he had been carrying around for the last forty-five years, was really catching up to him. As he walked down the sidewalk, he was thinking about how many times he started a diet, but every time, when he sat down to eat, "poof," like magic, all the food, drinks and desert, disappeared.

Now that he was retired, he didn't burn all those carbs like he used too. He never thought he would make it this far, after all. Some of his friends were dead already, between all of the cancer, heart attacks, strokes, diabetes and all the other bullshit caused from the lousy processed food and lack of exercise — who had a chance? He could feel his blood pressure rising now as he continued to walk. He had to calm himself down…at least that's what all his doctors told him.

He finally made it to the train station with a half hour to spare. He sat down to catch his breath and relax. The first thing that hit him was the smell of fresh popcorn. He looked around and spotted a vendor across the way. He had a large, red cart with a yellow and white striped umbrella over it. The sign on the cart read: "Soda and freshly-made Popcorn" He knew that would be his first stop. *Screw the doctors.*

He decided to go through security next and get that out of the way. Security was a real pain in the ass ever since the towers, the shootings, the bombings and all the rest of the evil bullshit. It took over twenty minutes to get through the line, which was packed and moving slowly. Finally, he made it back to the train platform. Now he could sit down, enjoy his "healthy lunch" and read his paper…

"Ahh…this is nice…just relax." He whispered to himself. He started reading the paper and daydreaming, which was his favorite pastime these days. Every now and then he would peek out from behind his paper, taking note of more and more people entering the platform area. They all came here for the "*Ride of a Lifetime;*" the Silver Streak Line. That's what it stated in all the newspapers, billboards, TV ads, and on the top of every Silver Streak train ticket.

"Yep, the ride of a lifetime," Dan said out loud.

He put his paper down and decided to read the info pack that came with his ticket. He opened the packet, the first card read; "a new concept in passenger trains! Speeds up to 300 miles per hour!" Dan kept reading on and on, "Departs New York City and has you in L.A., in less than 11 hours!" Dan continued to read, getting more excited with every detail.

"That's gotta be some kind of land speed record or something," he said out loud.

"What's that sir?" a lady asked, sitting next to him.

"Oh, nothing miss, just talking out loud," he replied. She smiled and went back talking with her son.

Dan loved trains ever since he was a little boy. He could still visualize his old Lionel Train as it chugged down the steel train tracks, puffing thick white smoke out of its stack, barely missing the lower limbs of the family Christmas tree. He remembered that smell of train oil, mixed with the scent of the spruce tree, along with Mom's turkey roasting in the oven. That thought brought back vivid memories of his childhood in the '50s. Those memories stayed with him forever. He would place his chin on the train platform, eye-to-eye with the train tracks. His big brother would sound the train whistle as the locomotive rounded the bend, chugging away. It made Dan jump ever time. Dan would love to go back in time and relive every minute of his childhood, while also retaining his collective wisdom…or would that ruin all the fun and the innocence of growing up? All of these thoughts and more were running through Dan's head today, and wondered why that was.

He was going to visit his daughter and her family in California. She was so persistent about having him visit that he couldn't say no. Besides that, he needed a change of scenery. He lived in Northeast Pennsylvania all of his life. He never traveled much, and that's how he got roped into this journey, in the first place. They teamed up on him, over the phone.

"Come on Dad, come out and visit with us,"

"Yeah Grandpa…come out…please…Please, please, please…", his two granddaughters chimed in.

"Okay, Dad, so you're coming, right?" his daughter, Jan, asked again.

"All right. If it will make you happy, I'll come," he chuckled, "When do you want me to come? What should I wear? What's the weather like?" After an hour of instructions from Jan, he was set to make the big trip.

So here he was, taking, *"the ride of a lifetime."* After he put away his ticket, he went back to reading his paper. He thought for sure that the lady sitting next to him must have thought there was something wrong with him, because she stared at him every time he talked to himself.

Hmmm, maybe she's right.

So this time, he would make an effort not to daydream, or talk to himself…

———

"NOT GUILTY." The judge declared, as he slammed down his gavel, on his hundred-year-old, oak bench.

The trial was finally over for Eli Washington, 38 years old, decorated war hero, turned private eye in the great city of

New York. It was a typical case gone wrong: hubby cheated on wife, wife wants revenge, wife hires private dick, hubby gets murdered, and everybody blames the dick.

Eli just wasted four months of his life on this bullshit case, not to mention the money wasted on his lawyer. He needed a vacation and some time to think. His buddy told him about the new train that ran from New York to L.A., which got Eli's attention. Soak up some sun, party out of town, maybe meet someone nice. There was nobody in Eli's life now. When he got back from duty, things went south with his now ex-wife. She wasn't good at waiting for him while he was in Iraq. A week after he deployed, she was in bed with his brother, and now that he thought about it, maybe even before then.

So he bought some new clothes, spent a few days with his mom, and got his ticket. At mom's house one evening, after a great homemade supper, he noticed a tear rolling down her cheek.

"Mom, you okay?"

"Sure honey, I just wish things could be like they used to be, you know, when your dad was with us and all."

"Me too, mom. I miss the old days a lot. Hey mom I've got a idea, why don't you come with me?"

"To California?…nooo…don't be silly, I could never go, too much to do around here, ya know?"

"Come on mom, you could use a vacation, I'll even buy a ticket for you, come on, what do you say?"

She shook her head no, and continued to wash the dishes.

"Well think about, okay mom?"

Eli didn't like to see his mom depressed. She didn't go with him, after all, but promised to have a big "shin-dig" when he got back from his vacation. The next day he kissed her goodbye and told her that he was going to bring her back a big present, something that she's always wanted…

"Come on Jimmy!" Sally Weeks shouted up the stairs to her son, in their two story, cape-cod home. It was the third time, in the past five minutes, that she tried to get his attention.

"We have to get moving or we're going to be late for the train!"

Jimmy heard her, but he was to busy saying goodbye to all of his bedroom friends. He was an only child. His parents tried for more, but mom had "complications," at least that's what he overheard one night when his parents were having a argument about it. But now he was leaving most of his precious belongings behind, and his little eight-year-old heart was breaking.

Mom was acting very strange ever since she woke up this morning. She kept him home from school, told him to pack as fast as he could, and only take what he absolutely needed to. And now she was shouting at him, to hurry up, every two minutes. He couldn't understand what was going on, and warm tears rolled out of his baby blue eyes, as he slowly packed his suitcase. He packed his PJ's, underwear, tooth brush, socks, and his favorite toy of all, G. I. Joe. Mom said there was no room for his toys but he didn't care, he was taking Joe, no matter what.

He looked up at his new TV set that he got for his birthday two weeks ago, and his PlayStation that was just below the TV on his dresser. There was a family photo of the three of them hanging on the wall, just to the right of the TV. Mom looked so pretty with her long blonde hair and dad had a crew cut, just like GI Joe's. Jimmy loved that picture. He looked at his model cars that he and his Dad built together, and also his dinosaur collection. He didn't want to leave any of it behind. Kneeling on the floor now, trying to hold back his tears, he slowly looked around his small room, one last time.

His wooden toy box sat over in the corner, with a broken hinge on the right-hand side. Dad promised to fix it as soon as he got the time. His little antique desk and chair, that mom bought at a yard sale, stood next to the toy box. He must have drawn and colored a million pictures on his desk. Then he looked at his unmade, warm, cozy bed, with its over-stuffed pillow, where he would lay and dream about traveling the world on a pirate ship. He wiped the tears from his eyes and looked out his window that had at least eight coats of white paint on it and a cracked pane of glass in the upper right-hand corner. On stormy nights, the wind would whistle through the crack and whisper many things to him.

"Jimmy, let's go right NOW!"

"Okay MOM. Give me one more second!" He yelled down the stairs.

"Go Jimmy, go," a faint voice whispered to him. Jimmy jumped, turned and looked around for the intruder, but it was just the wind, whistling through the crack.

"Who's there?" He questioned, and started shaking…

"Be safe Jimmy, be safe."

He looked around one more time for that raspy voice. His heart jumped. He snatched his backpack, ran out of his room, down the stairs and into his mother's arms.

"Let's go Mom, I'm ready to go now!" She grabbed her two bags and they both ran out of the house, across the porch and headed for the car. They placed their bags in the back seat and jumped into the front.

"Buckle up, sweetie." she said, as she looked at him. She reached over and brushed back the hair from his eyes and saw the tears running down his cheeks. She started to cry too, remembering what her husband did to her last night, and what she did to him, in the heat of the fight.

In the past six months things got out of hand a lot. he would come home, half drunk and fight with her almost every night. He had a drinking problem. There was no getting around it, and he wasn't going to stop. Usually he would slap her around and call her filthy names, then pass out on the bed. Not last night. The slaps turned into punches and the name calling turned into rape. Sally tried to fight him off, but he easily overpowered her small frame. He brutally took what he wanted and wasn't going to stop. While he was on top of her, she reached over to her night stand and grabbed a pair of scissors out of the drawer and stabbed him right in the throat. He couldn't comprehend why he was gagging at first. He was going into shock. Sally tried to roll him off of her as his blood was pouring onto her chest and face. She couldn't scream out, in fear of waking Jimmy or, worse, bringing the cops to the murder scene. At least that's what she thought it was…murder…all she knew was, she had to get this pig off of her…

"Aren't we waiting for Daddy?" Jimmy asked, snapping Sally out of her thoughts.

"I'm sorry, honey, but we have to leave right now, before your father gets home from work." She lied, trying to hold back the tears and collect herself. She had to be strong. She leaned over and gave Jimmy a reassuring hug. He reached around her, and returned the hug, making her wince in pain. Every part of her body was in agony, especially her abdomen and ribs.

"Do you have everything that I told you to pack, honey?" Sally asked.

Jimmy nodded.

"Good, so let's get going, okay sweetie?" She turned the key, in the old Chevy…click…click…click…

"Oh shit, you gotta be kidding me!" she cursed under her breath. "Come on, start you son of a bitch!" She turned the key again…this time it started right up. She popped the shifter into drive, and hit the gas pedal. She gave Jimmy a big smile, and squeezed his tiny hand. They left their home for the last time, not knowing what the future would bring.

The train station loud speakers crackled and then came to life. "Train 438 now boarding platform 2B. Boston and all points east, boarding now, departing in twenty minutes. Train 438 now..."

"OW!," Dan said, as he looked up from reading his paper. He saw a little boy running around the bench and he was coming around for a second lap. As he rounded Dan's curve, he stepped on Dan's foot again, for the second time.

"Whoa sonny!" he said, as he reached out with his arm to slow the kid down.

"Oh sorry mister, I didn't mean to step on your feet." He yelled back, as he kept running past Dan. Then he stumbled over someone's suitcase and down he went! Dan jumped up off the bench and helped the boy get up.

"Are you alright son?" Dan asked, as he dusted the kid off.

"Yes sir, "He replied, "sorry about your feet."

"That's okay pal," Dan laughed, "I only use the bottoms of them anyway."

The kid gave Dan a puzzled look, and Dan figured he didn't get his joke. He took off again like a cat. As he came around the bench for the third time, Dan yelled out, "Don't call me sir, it makes me feel old...well older than I am anyway." Dan laughed at himself and thought, "*me, old? I don't think so.*"

"What should I call you then?" He asked.

"Just call me Dan. What's your name?"

The child slowed down and finally stopped.

"Jimmy, Jimmy Weeks."

Dan held out his hand and Jimmy shook it.

"Nice to meet you Jimmy."

A woman's voice yelled out, "Jimmy don't be bothering the nice man."

Dan turned towards the voice and saw a very good looking woman, blonde hair, maybe 5'4", pretty blue eyes, and
great smile. She couldn't be a day over thirty five and maybe
weighed 120 pounds. *"Not too bad"* Dan thought.

"He's all right, ma'am," Dan stated, "Just having a little
fun." Dan's eyes met hers, then she quickly looked down at
the floor.

"Sometimes I think I should just put a harness on him,"
she said laughing a little bit, "He's so active."

"You should be happy he is. Most kids these days just
want to play on their cell phones or play games all day long,
while there stuffing their face with junk food." Dan walked
over and extended his hand out.

"My name is Dan Jensen."

"Sally Weeks, she replied and shook Dan's hand meekly.
She managed a smile and sat down, while keeping an eye
on Jimmy, and her other eye on their luggage. She looked at
Dan again and added,

"Thank you for not getting angry with Jimmy, he can get
on your nerves real fast sometimes." She gave Dan a nervous
smile and didn't look him in the eye.

"Don't be silly, he seems like a great kid."

"I guess you're going on '*the ride of a lifetime,*' right?"
She asked.

"Yeah, I'm going out to visit my daughter and her family"

"Well that sounds very nice." Sally said with a slight smile.
Dan thought she looked nervous about something. "We can't
wait to get out of this city."

"Oh, and why is that?" Dan asked.

She looked at her watch, then looked back at Jimmy, and
then back at Dan, who was still waiting for her answer.

"Ahh, what were you saying?" She asked, as she looked for
Jimmy, who was taking another lap around the platform bench.

"Nothing, nothing important." Dan stated, thinking she had things on her mind, so he discontinued their conversation. He looked at his watch. Twenty more minutes to go before boarding.

"Phil, do you want something to eat before you leave for work?" Clara Dawson asked her husband of thirty five years.

"Just a sandwich, honey. Grilled cheese and tomato, if it isn't a bother." Phil yelled from the bathroom.

He was performing his morning ritual of shaving the old fashion way. Warm, steaming air filled the cozy bathroom. He soaked his face with a hot, damp towel, holding it in place with both hands. Then he lathered up his cheeks and chin with hot, thick shaving cream using his old shaving brush and cup that his father left him when he passed away ten years ago.

He had to keep wiping the fogged mirror every so often to see how he was doing. He didn't mind that at all, because he loved shaving this way. It gave him pleasant memories of watching his father shave many years ago. He would sit in the bathroom on top of a old wooden clothes hamper, leaning against the towel rack that was barely secured to the wall. He would ask his dad a million questions, lots of silly questions, he thought now, but back then they were important to him. His dad would answer most of them one way or another. The questions got a little bit more difficult when Phil became a teenager.

"Phil! Are you ready for your sandwich yet?" Clara yelled into the bathroom. Phil jumped slightly and snapped out of his day dreaming.

"Give me five more minutes honey." Phil was a very happy man, married to a wonderful wife. Two great kids. Well, they weren't kids anymore, they were both in their late thirty's now and married. Very nice home and a job he loved.

He worked for the railroad for the past forty years. Started out as an oiler and worked his way up to senior engineer. Now he was the engineer for the fastest train in the country, *The Silver Streak*. He loved piloting The Silver Streak. It had a fully automatic drive train, unlimited horse power and a smooth-as-silk riding experience. Every morning, before he would board her, he would have to do a pre-drive inspection. Phil would make his way down through the interior of the car, checking safety gear, while making notes on his tablet computer check list. He'd test the fire extinguishers, emergency lighting, stop pulls, and more. He'd walk all the way to the rear of the car and check that all service equipment was secured to the floor mounts. When passing the mini-fridge, he would reach in and grab a soda. Then he would return to the front of the car and go outside, walk onto the loading platform, taking several steps before turning around to admire the giant marvel.

"What a beauty," he would think. Twelve feet tall, polished stainless steel skin, as sleek as a silver bullet. It reminded him of a jumbo jet without the wings. He would walk back over and attach his tablet computer to a port, just to the left of the boarding door. It would scan the entire car, checking off all systems, then, once it completed its task, the screen would flash, *"all systems go."* Finally, Phil would climb aboard and place the tablet in his brief case.

Phil snapped back to reality. He wiped off his freshly shaven face, then slapped on some Old Spice aftershave, and rubbed his hands over his checks.

"Smooth as a baby's ass," he said out loud, and chuckled, thinking that his father used to say the same thing.

He exited the warm, steamy bathroom, grabbed his

overnight bag off the bed and headed for the kitchen.

"Oh Phil, you smell so nice! Is that the after shave I bought you for your birthday?"

"Yes it is dear. Is my sandwich ready?"

Clara nodded.

He sat down at the table and dug into his meal.

"Honey, this is the best toasted cheese sandwich you've ever made." Phil mumbled to Clara with his mouth full.

"Phil, don't talk with your mouth full or you're going to choke," Clara said laughing, and shaking her head.

He started laughing and then almost did choke. After he finished his meal, he gave Clara a big hug and told her that he would see her in a couple days. He went outside, got into his car, and backed out of the driveway. Just before he backed onto the street, he looked at his home. He wasn't sure why, but he felt a strong urge to pause a moment to soak it all in...green wooden shutters, hanging on the pale, yellow wood siding, that needed a paint job, and a small circular white brick porch, with two white columns, supporting a green shingled roof...he loved his house and his life, with his beautiful wife...

"See you soon, Clara..."

Dan almost dropped his newspaper, when he heard the bellowing blast from the air horn of the Silver Streak. It rounded the corner like a giant, silver, rocket ship and came into full view for everyone to admire. The PA system came alive once again:

"Ten minutes to boarding of the new Silver Streak. Please have your tickets and your IDs ready for boarding"

People were getting super excited now, gazing at this exquisite, futuristic train, including Dan and Jimmy.

"This is it, the big ride! *The Ride of a Lifetime!*" Dan exclaimed. He was really jacked up now. The air horn blasted again, then the train came to a complete stop. Dan stood there, eyes wide open. Jimmy was jumping up and down like a mad man! His eyes were as wide as saucers. He started to move closer towards the train,

"Mom, Mom," he yelled, "MOM here it is!, LOOK MOM, look!"

"Yes, Jimmy, I see it, it's very nice." She stated, without much enthusiasm. Dan moved over towards Jimmy and jumped into a conversation with him.

"She's a beauty, isn't she Jimmy?"

Jimmy eyes where gleaming just as much as much as Dan's. Dan knelt down so he could enjoy the view from Jimmy's perspective. From here the train looked twenty feet tall, it looked super aerodynamic and sleek. The front was like a polished steel missile, with a wrap-around, tinted glass windshield. The boarding door and the side windows were also tinted, making it hard to see inside. A blue and gold vinyl stripe started at ground level, just behind the boarding door and made their way up the side of the car at a fifty-degree angle, stopping at a eight feet high. From there they were parallel with the ground and went all the way to the back of the car.

"That must be why they call it the silver streak," Jimmy stated, "Right Dan? Because of all the shiny steel and that long streak?"

"I guess so, partner. It looks that way."

People where very excited now, between the grand entrance, blasting of the air horn and little kids running all around…it was getting very noisy and crowded . Finally the door opened! The conductor stepped out first and then the engineer…

"ALL ABOARD! ALL ABOARD!" he shouted. Dan and Jimmy were already standing at the front of the line. They side stepped to their right and peeked inside.

"I can't wait to get aboard!" Dan said excitedly. "How about you, Jimmy?"

"WOW ! Check out those controls Dan," Jimmy squealed.

"And how 'bout those fancy seats Jimmy. They look just like Lazy Boy recliners!"

The conductor politely reached out to Dan and Jimmy and stated,

"Tickets please,"

Dan reached into his shirt pocket and handed him his packet.

"Just your ticket sir, and your ID."

Dan got that embarrassed look again, like he had earlier at he subway exit. He fumbled with his wallet, almost dropping it, then finally handed the conductor his license and ticket.

"Thank you Sir, you can board now."

Dan was ecstatic, he quickly reached down, picked up his bag and started to board the train.

"Don't forget your license Sir." the conductor said, handing back Dan's ID.

"Oh, yeah, sorry about that." He reached out and took it, turned and stepped aboard.

"*The ride of a lifetime,*" he thought. He couldn't wait. This was going to be great! He loved trains all of his life, and this one was brand new.

Sally was picking up their luggage with difficulty. She looked for Jimmy to help her, then she heard his yell.

"Come on Mom! Let's get on now!" He was yelling at the top of his lungs.

She spotted him at the front of the line, right next to the conductor.

"Wait for me kiddo!" She yelled back, "and give me some help with the bags."

"Come on mom, I don't want to lose my place in line."

"Just wait right there," she said, dragging the luggage across the platform. When she finally made it to the front of the line, she dropped the bags down and dug through her purse for the tickets. By this time she was pretty stressed out.

"Here's our tickets sir, and my ID." she said, handing them to the conductor. People around her were getting a little frustrated by now, with the hold up, that Jimmy had caused. She handed Jimmy his backpack, picked up her suite cases,and told him to get aboard. She gave him *the look*, and he knew enough not to push her any further.

Jerry and Patti Cooper were running as fast as their legs would allow them. They positively had to make the train station on time.

According to Jerry's watch, they were running late. Patti's blue eyes were full of tears and she was sniffing more and more as they ran, probably due to her asthma. Patti's broken heart warned her that they had to get the hell out of this city immediately. Her brother's pace was hard to keep up with, as they ran for their lives.

Jerry was 17 years-old, fair-haired, blue-eyed, and athletically-built. Patti was his twin, but she wasn't in as good of shape as he was, so she was lagging behind. She started coughing and gasping now and was slowing down even more.

"Jerry, stop for a minute!" she gasped, "Please Jerry, I can't breath! "

"Come on, sis, we gotta keep moving!" He shouted over his shoulder.

"I need to stop! Just stop and let me use my inhaler, okay?"

Jerry loved his sister with all of his heart, so he stopped, turned around and gave her a hug.

"I'm sorry sis." He stated softly and continued to hug her. "I'm real sorry." He backed up a little. "Go ahead sis, get your inhaler out and take a break." He noticed a bench just a few feet up the street.

"Come on sis, let's sit down over there and take a minute. They made their way to the bench and sat down. Patti dug her inhaler out of her shoulder bag and took a deep hit on it. After another dose, her breathing started to ease up a little. She looked over at Jerry and smiled.

"Thanks Jere, I'm feeling a little better now."

"Take your time sis, relax a little bit and then we'll go." Jerry was still anxious to get moving but knew she needed a break. He looked across the street at the old buildings and the people walking up and down the dirty sidewalks.

He started to relax a little and his thoughts started drifting. He thought back to the time, not long ago, when they planned this escape.

They saved ever penny that they earned for the last two years to pay for this trip. They skipped eating their school lunches and got part-time jobs when and where they could find them. Patti worked at Mickey-D's and took on baby sitting jobs. Jerry mowed lawn's, washed cars, at the local Brite-Shine car wash and ran earns for the elderly neighbors. They kept their money in a secret hiding place under the outside stairs, beneath a broken slab of weathered concrete. They had purchased the tickets two months ago and carefully made detailed plans. Patti made up a modest budget for all their needs. Five hundred dollars for the tickets, eight hundred dollars for food and lodging and three hundred dollars for emergencies. Jerry kept the emergency money tucked in his worn out Nike's. Patti kept the rest in her shoulder bag. They had prepared for everything and today was the big day to get out of town and away from their parents.

If their so-called parents ever found out about the money or suspected their plans to run away, they would have punish them both severely or even something worse.

"Let's get going," Patti urged, "I'm feeling much better now. Jerry was startled a little from his thoughts. He jumped up, checked his watch, and held out his hand for Patti.

"Okay sis, let's get moving."

They kept a pretty good pace as they headed for the train station. As they moved along, Patti started reflecting back on the past. Her childhood had been so screwed up that it was agonizing just to remember it. She desperately wanted *not* to remember. She was around six or seven years old the night her father quietly entered her bedroom late one night and softly spoke her name several times.

"Patti...Patti...Patti...it's Daddy, honey, can you hear me... sweetie? You were crying honey," she remembered his voice, which he kept very low. He continued, "are you alright honey?"

He slowly reached out and touched her shoulder, and leaned closer. "Come here sweetie, let me hold you baby. I'll make it better."

Reliving this memory made Patti feel sick, and temporarily paralyzed her. She tried not to think about it, but once it took hold in her mind, she'd relive the experience in real time, unable to move or breath.

"Now sweetie this will be our little secret okay? Mommy or nobody else would understand and if you tell anyone, daddy will get into trouble and I know you wouldn't want that, would you?"

She remembered the emptiness that followed. She looked around her room. She stared at her favorite doll, Soffie, with her green dress and white laced apron. Her hand-made bed spread with matching pillow case that her mom made. All her stuffed animals lined up across the top of her dresser, tomorrow's school outfit hanging on the closet door. Everything was so perfectly in its place…perfect…she grabbed and held Soffie tightly, and eventually fell asleep.

Patti remembered telling her mother what happened. Her mother got angry and called her a liar. The nightly visits kept happening. What was an empty feeling turned into a recurring cold and breathless nightmare. The day came when she found out Jerry was also being visited by their father at night. That's when they made the plan to escape from their nightmare.

"Catch up sis!" Jerry yelled over his shoulder!

Snapping her out of her memories. "There's the train station! We made it. We finally made it!" he yelled. Tears poured out of his eyes, but he had the biggest smile in the world on his face. "We did it sis, we did it!"

"I can't believe we've made it, Jere. We're really going to get out of here." She was so choked up, she could hardly catch her breath. She cried for herself and for her brother. They held hands as they ran over the loading platform.

"We're free Jerry, free at last." Patti panted out the words, she needed her inhaler, she was out of breath from all the running and excitement.

They handed the conductor their tickets,

"You just made it kids," he stated, with a smile. They gave each other a hug and a kiss and boarded The Silver Streak. Patti felt all the repulsive and dreadful past being lifted from her shoulders as they walked down the isle to their assigned seats.

"Nothing but good times from now on sis, right?"

CHAPTER 2

THE RIDE OF A LIFETIME

The engineer was at the door now. He climbed up three steps and looked around at his excited passengers, gave a smile and a nodded his head. He grabbed the waist line of his trousers and pulled them up, over his belly, and tucked his shirt in (when he did this around his grandchildren they would call him "old-fashioned"). He slipped into the pilot seat. It was super comfortable and had the fragrance of new leather. He loved his seat. He started his pre-trip check by scanning his index finger on the screen. The surrounding screens lit up like a Christmas tree, immediately getting Jimmy's attention. The first thing Phil adjusted, was the air conditioning in his seat, then he adjusted the position of the seat, he loved fact that it had over twenty one different settings. Jimmy kept looking at the control panel, getting more and more excited as Phil continued to touch prompts, making more lights pop up, as well as sounds. He had to get a closer look at this wonderful marvel. With out asking permission, he got out of his seat and made his way to the driver, peered over his shoulder and started asking a million questions. Sally was ready to cozy up with a good book and notice Jimmy was missing. She jumped up with a slight fear in her eyes, she was getting ready to holler at Jimmy…when Dan stood up and ran interference,

"Take it easy Sally, he's right there," he said, pointing to Jimmy, "he's just looking at all the lights."

Being a little embarrassed, Sally started to laugh, she lifted her hand to her mouth while shaking her head and laughed out loud.

"I feel so silly." She giggled.

"Don't feel like that," Dan stated, "It's good to see you laugh, you look like you needed one."

She looked up at Dan and said "You're very good with Jimmy, he usually doesn't warm up to strangers, especially men."

She looked over at Jimmy who was still yapping away with the driver. Lowering her voice and leaning towards Dan, she added, "His father wasn't the kindest man around, if you know what I mean."

"Yeah, I can relate to that," Dan said, acknowledging her, with a nod. "My father was pretty strict with me when I was growing up." Dan was thinking, *"she was a very nice, down to earth type…"* Jimmy was starting to get a little loud…

"I'll get him for you Sally." Dan said, turning towards Jimmy and stepped forward,

"Hey partner, what's up?"

"Aww Dan, this is the coolest, come on, check this out." Jimmy hollered, he was totally mesmerized. "Rad, isn't".

"Ah, I guess so?" Dan said laughing, "Don't you want to sit back down now, pal? Maybe the driver needs a break from all of your questions, so he can finish his job."

The driver looked up, "Oh he's OK, I don't mind, I enjoy the company, by the way, my name is Phil…Phil Dawson…" he stated, holding his hand and shook hands with Dan.

THE RIDE OF A LIFETIME

"Dan Jensen, glad to meet you Phil, and this is Jimmy Weeks, my new best friend, right Jimmy?"

"You bet Dan." Jimmy stated, with a big grin.

"Well it's good to meet both of you," Phil said, reaching over to shake Jimmy's hand. "I guess you could grab your seats, if you want to get going."

"You don't have to ask me twice," Jimmy replied, "Let's get this *Silver Monster*, rolling, right Dan?"

"Right Jimmy," Thinking that was an odd thing to say, "*Silver Monster.*"

"Remember to buckle up, guys" Phil said as they went to their seats.

Dan's seat was in the front row, just to the right of the Phil. What a view he had, the window's appeared larger from the inside and you couldn't notice the tinting at all, because from the exterior they appeared very dark. Jimmy and his mom sat in the second row to his left. Each row contained six seats, three on each side of the isle. Dan only had two seats because of the door. Directly behind him was an older couple, maybe in their mid 70's, he guessed. Dan said hello to them and smiled. They waved and smiled back. He stretched and a yawn as he scanned the car, it was almost full. A lot of couples, some kids, a group of guy's in suite's about half way back, already tipping a few. Two servers going up and down the isle, passing out canned soda, coffee, and little bottles of "happy juice". He spotted four or five guy's, in the back of the car, with NFL jersey's on, getting a little loud. Must be going to the big game, he thought. For the most part, they all looked like a nice bunch of people, he thought, as he sat down. Then he started shooting the breeze with Phil,

"So Phil, are we ready to get started?"

"Almost Dan, we have one more passenger that we're waiting on. He must be pretty important to delay us, it's never happened before." He added.

"I'll bet you enjoy this job, don't you?" Dan asked, changing the subject.

"Oh yeah, this will be my third cross country run, wait till you see what this baby can do Dan." Phil's voice was full of excitement. You could see it all over his face, his big broad smile revealed a small, angled scar on his left upper lip (it reminded Dan of Elvis). His green/blue eyes, were over shadowed by big bushy, grey eyebrows. Dan glanced out the side window, and noticed the loading platform was empty, with the exception of the porter lifting a couple of suitcases into the loading bin. Just then, the speaker on the control panel buzzed...

"Your clear to depart Phil."..."Roger that, what about that VIP we've been waiting for?" Phil shot back..."I guess he's a no show."

"Well Dan, time to get to work." Phil stated while tapping a few more apps. He checked the door pressure, then slowly brought up the amps by pushing the joystick forward. He started to release the brake It was a large, yellow, T-shaped handle, just to right of the joystick.

"Hold it Phil," Dan chuckled, looking out the side window, "I think your missing VIP is trying to get your attention."

Phil pulled back on the joy stick, dropping the revving engine, and locked the brakes. Jimmy gave out a disappointing sigh. The stranger ran up to the door and banged on the glass with a anxious look on his face. Phil open the door and it almost pushed the VIP backwards. He sprung into the car and climbed the steps in one bound, handing Phil his ticket in one motion. Phil took the ticket with a smile, he checked it, and asked for ID. Then he pointed to the back,

"Your seat is halfway back on the right, just below the emergency skylight sign."

"Thank you Sir," he said, not offering any apology for his

tardiness and headed back. "ALL ABOARD!," the Conductor's voice called through all of the speakers, including the one on the front panel. Phil smiled once again and started to rev her up.

Hitting the intercom, Phil started his departure speech. "Attention all passengers, make sure you are all seated and your luggage is secured. For your convenience you have individual, entertainment pods on the back of each seat, complete with Sony headphones, TV, Game and movie service." Phil released the E-brake and slid the joystick forward, the 15,000/hp engine came to life. Phil looked at Dan and smiled...

"Hang on Dan, it's time to rock and roll." They slowly cruised out of the station and a few minutes later they switched tracks to the main line. The tracks of the main line were so new that the sunlight reflected off of them, like glass. Dan remembered reading in the *"Silver Streak"* packet, the one that came with his ticket, it stated that the (*New/Cal)* railway installed over three thousand miles of new rails, costing over a billion dollars...The engine wined a little louder. Dan could see the speedometer from his seat, 45mph, ...55, ...65 ...The train was picking up speed fast, 75, ...85, ...In a couple of seconds. Dan was truly impressed, After five short minutes they were doing 195 mph. Just then, another announcement came over the intercom system,

"Attention all passengers, when we reach 220 mph, your window's will automatically tint down, preventing your exterior view." Some people gave out a disappointed gasp, and look a little worried. Before they could make any comments, the message continued, "It is for your own safety. Studies have shown that, at high speeds, looking out at the passing landscape can cause nausea and severe headaches." Disappointed groans were now turning into verbal remarks...

"Note: you can view the exterior through the front

windshield or use your personal option, to view it on your own viewing screen, by pressing, (app #34); Thank you for your cooperation of this matter."

210…215…220…windows started to darken…230…240.

"Holy shit," Dan whispered, "this bitch can kick some ass."

Phil smiled as he pushed the joy stick to 65 percent full power. Dan looked at the tracks, the railroad ties were coming at them so fast, that they looked like a strobe light. Dan's stomach started to churn, and he felt like he would upchuck any second. He quickly closed his eyes…he remembered back to the fastest speed he had ever gone, …it was the time, in his old 240-Z. He had been cruising around 90 mph, burning up I-81, coming home from a Penn State game. Some fancy-ass dudes pulled along side of him in a new, turbocharged Mustang. They started laughing at him and flipped him off, he dumped the clutch and dropped the Z into 4th gear, put the pedal to the metal and it was on! He hit 145 mph in a few seconds. The dudes were gaining on him, he speed shifted to 5th and the Z hugged the ground better than a 'Vette …155 …160 …165 ! He checked his rearview, and could barely see the Mustang. Suddenly the Z began shaking and drifting and he backed off. No sign of the Mustang — guess the boys shit themselves …

Back in train, 245 mph. "Boy, Phil, is it always this smooth?" 255 mph.

"Yes — isn't amazing Dan? Smooth as silk, *'the ride of a lifetime.'*"

265 mph. "Well, I'm impressed" Dan added as he looked out the darkened window. He squinted, trying to see through the tint. Everything was a blur: houses, trees, and towns zoomed by so quickly that he could not comprehend any of it. He started to getting woozy again and that took the edge off his excitement. He shifted his view to the floor, put his

hand under his chin and composed his spinning head. After a few minutes, he started to feel like his old self. 275mph. He looked around and there was Jimmy, staring at him.

"Hi Dan, you feeling alright?"

"Yes Jimmy, I'm fine." he lied, not wanting to appear looking like a wimp, "and you, how are you doing?"

"I'm fine Dan. Hey, check out the ceiling, all shiny steel," Jimmy said looking up, "and these seats, Dan, look at all the things they do,"

Without waiting for Dan to answer, Jimmy started to press multiple buttons, making the seat do a little dance.

"Jimmy, stop that," Sally cried out, "you're going to break the seat."

Dan smiled at Jimmy and Sally. Dan started looking around the coach, and gave Jimmy a reassuring grin. He looked up at the ceiling and studied it. It appeared to be very well constructed. It was polished stainless steel, welded together at the joints, which looked approximately eight foot apart. Then he set his attention on the seats. They were first class, soft and comfy, plenty of leg room, even for his large frame. You controlled them with a handheld remote pad that had over twenty positions. Dan thought; *"what a marvel, the craftsmanship seems flawless."*

Dan felt like he was in heaven. He made a few adjustments to his seat, smiled and closed his eyes and enjoyed the ride…*"The ride of a life time"* …after a few seconds, he reached into his overnight bag and took out his favorite read, *"The Stand"* by Stephen King, opening it up to page 406, he found his place, where he left off and continued to read. He had read this novel at least five times but he still loved to take that journey with Stu and the others. He was so comfortable in his seat that he began to doze off. His book slipped from his grasp and he jumped slightly and managed to snagged it before it fell. He grinned and continued to read. His mind started to wandered again...*ride of a lifetime...I promise ...*

"LOOK OUT!"

"Eeeeaaahhhhh!"

"HELP ME!"

Dan struggled to wake up.

"WHAT?" Dan shouted, still groggy, "What the hell is going on?" Screams came from everywhere! Then a sudden jerk brought him totally out of his slumber. Phil cried out,

"HELP ME!"

Dan looked at Phil struggling with the brake control lever. He was pulling back on it with all his strength! He looked over at Dan, his eyes bulging with terror,

"DAN! Help me! Please help me!"

Dan jumped up, but was slammed back down as the car swayed to the right. He made a second effort to stand up again...

"Is this a nightmare?" he thought. He tried moving towards Phil but his body didn't respond.

"This has to be a goddamn nightmare" he said while shaking his head.

Phil was pulling so hard on the T-handle brake that the veins in his arms were bulging out like nightcrawlers, and sweat was pouring down his red face. Dan forced himself to move ahead and was reaching out to help Phil. He felt some strange force pushing him back and keeping him from assisting Phil.

Dan grabbed the brake handle...it seemed even larger now. He blinked his eyes and shook his head, thinking that he was hallucinating. Grabbing the brake along with Phil, they pulled as hard as they could.

"IT'S NOT SLOWING DOWN DAN!" he screamed.

Dan lifted one leg up and planted on the front panel board. He pushed with all his strength and pulled with his whole upper body. Dan looked out through the windshield. Small trees and bushes were deflecting off the front and sides of the train. Dirt, rocks, and debris were hitting and spinning away, looking like a small tornado. Everything around Dan went into slow motion. Screams were coming from behind him and they were intensifying every second. He thought of little Jimmy. He took a quick glance back to look for him.

"PULL DAN, PULL!" Phil shouted!

"Help me, help me..." Was that little Jimmy? Dan looking back again at Jimmy's seat.

"PULL, DAN! PULL THE FUCKING BRAKE!" Dan gave it all he had, for the second time. The Speeding Silver Streak finally began to slow down.

Trees were being torn apart everywhere. Phil glanced at the speedometer: 255 mph.

"Way too fast, Dan...Jesus!" Phil shouted, "Sweet Jesus." Looking out again, Dan witnessed a blizzard of dust, sand, pebbles and stones, smashing into the windshield and scattering like buckshot, from a double barrel shotgun.

"220 miles per hour," Dan yelled as he was glaring out through the windshield and the raging dust storm

"Phil, look! NO MORE TRACKS!"

Phil quickly raised his head, and peered out through windshield at the dust and rocks.

"Looks like the tracks end in about five hundred feet !" He hollered back at Dan.

Dan noticed Phil's face was deep red, his forehead was drenched with sweat, dripping down into his now closed eyes.

"You okay Phil?"

"Yeah, just keep pulling! Pull Dan!"

165 mph. They were both out of steam. They had nothing left. Dan's arms where killing him. Phil started to loose his grip.

120mph. Dan tried to yelled out again, but nothing came

out. Phil seeing the expression on Dan's face cried out,

"What's wrong?" Dan still couldn't speak. His weakened hands, slipped off the brake handle for a split second! And he pointed outside...

"Oh My GOD ! The tracks are gone!" Phil gasped and went into full panic mode. Just then the brake lever snapped!

85mph. The train started digging into the earth. Dan flew forward smashing into the windshield like a giant bug on a hot, summer night. Then he ricocheted onto the floor. He felt a sharp pain instantly in his back. He couldn't stand up because of the negative G-force created by the deceleration of the train.

40 mph. Laying on the floor he looked to Phil for help. Phil was still strapped into his safety harness.

"Sorry, buddy...can't...heeellllllppp!" The windshield shattered — it sounded like a sonic boom. A large tree limb blasted through, piercing Phil's chest.

25 mph. The train flipped to the left. Windows and luggage compartments started popping and suite cases and bags were falling all over the place. The car was totally on its side now, sliding to a complete, twisted stop.

0 mph. The stainless steel ceiling was ripped wide open, exposing electrical wires and metal tubing. Sparks were flying and gases were leaking into the car. Passengers were falling out of their seats from the left side of the car and dropping down onto passengers who were on right side. Clouds of dust were now inside the car mixing with the smell of burning wires and toxic gas. Panic was in full mode! Choking, coughing, screaming and cursing was all that could be heard.

Dan tried to get up off the floor but his back was killing him. He rolled over onto his stomach and pushed himself up into a kneeling position. That's when he realized that the train was on it's side. He sat down and looked up at Phil...

"Oh my God Phil," he cried out, "Phil, …Phil…" The tree branch went right through Phil's chest and protruded out of his back and through his seat. Dark, red blood was dripping everywhere! It worked its way down Phil's arm onto the large branch and then, smaller branches, and leaves, finally hitting the floor just to the left of where Dan was now sitting.

Phil's face was also covered in thick blood that was laced with hundreds of glass chips from the windshield. Dan's eyes watered up. He became oblivious to all of the chaos around him. He closed his eyes and said a prayer. As he opened his eyes, Phil moved, or at least Dan thought he did. Phil's eyes were wide open now and looking straight at Dan. *That eerie feeling came back again. Like before, on the subway stairs.* Phil was staring at him, and Dan started shaking all over. He couldn't move.

"*Dan,*" *Phil hissed.* "*Dan, save yourself. Get the fuck out, Dan… before it's to late…*"

He could hardly hear Phil through all of the choking and wheezing.

"*Save yourself Dan…or you will end up in Hell.*"

Dan was terrified. His gut was killing him. He was pouring sweat.

"What the fuck is that supposed to mean?"

He looked up at Phil again, he had a four-inch gash in the middle of his forehead. His teeth were smashed inward, chipped and broken right off. Blood and glass oozed down over his bottom lip, and over his clean-shaven chin and then dropping down to mix with his blood on the tree limb. His face was the color of death…Dan knew that Phil was totally dead. He saw Phil's eyes were closed, not bulging or opened, and those bloody lips were definitely not moving.

He was dead…just dead.

Dan managed to look up at the sky through the shattered passenger windows. Smoke and sparks swirled throughout the car, mixing with the panic screams of the passengers. He moved his attention to the front view of the car. Through all of the dust he saw the sun starting it's decent into the sky. He felt the warm rays on his face, giving him hope, for a split second. He turned around and looked at the back of the car. Screams had turned into moaning and crying. Wires hung down, like long black snakes, hissing and sparking. It reminded him of lit fuses on a row of black-cat, fire crackers.

"Jimmy, Jimmy, where are you!" Sally cried out, with a painful voice. Dan moved towards her and reached out to help her up.

"Sally it's me, Dan, are you alright?"

"I'm okay Dan, just a few scratches and a burning pain in my leg. Do you see Jimmy anywhere?"

"Down here Mom," Jimmy replied, with a groan. Dan reached down and carefully got Jimmy to his feet.

"Are you okay, Jimmy?" Sally asked.

"Yes, Mom," he answered, as he reached for her and gave her a big hug. She grimaced in pain from her old injuries and now new ones.

"Oh Mom, are you hurt?"

"Just a little honey."

"We gotta get out of here," Dan suggested,

"I agree, but how, Dan?" Sally asked.

Jimmy pointed to the windshield and suggested, "Maybe through there?"

"No Jimmy, too much broken glass and tree branches."

"I've gotta get out of here!" some guy shouted, as he made his from the back of the car, pushing and shoving anyone who got in his way. When the guy made it to where they were standing, Dan stepped in front of Sally and Jimmy and held his arm's out to protect them.

"Get out of the way, fat ass — I'm going through that

window!" He was a very large, well built young man. He was one of the guys, who were wearing the NFL jerseys. Dan also noticed he was carrying something in his right hand. Dan kept quiet, he knew better then to say anything at this time. He was no match for this bruiser. The guy pushed by Dan and went directly to the windshield, got into a batting stance...

CRASH! Right through the semi-broken windshield. Chips of glass flew everywhere. He kept swinging at it, until it was all cleared off.

"Holy shit, Dan!" Jimmy yelled out. "He really did have a baseball bat." Dan couldn't believe it.

"It's a good thing I didn't try to stop him." Dan said with a nervous laugh.

"Jimmy you watch your mouth!" Sally said in a firm voice. The big guy started to make his escape, snapping off small limbs and branches, that got into his way. Dan was thinking, "*this guy is a maniac...but he is getting the job done.*"

"Let's go guys," Dan said turning towards Sally and Jimmy. "Give me a hand Jimmy, you take her right hand and I'll take her left." They gently guided Sally towards the front of the coach.

"Okay Sally, you have to bend down a little bit to make it under the window." Dan cautioned, "Keep her steady Jimmy, watch her back." Jimmy nodded nervously.

"I will Dan. Are you all right, Mom?"

"Yes honey, I'll make it."

They finally worked their way out through the tree limbs and felt the warm sunshine glow on their faces.

"Let's set her down over here pal, on that rock."

"Okay Dan," Jimmy responded as they slowly lowered her down.

"Thank God we are off of that steel coffin," Sally blurted out.

That's a strange thing to say, Dan thought.

Jimmy sat down next to his mom, looked at Dan and said, "Aren't you going to sit down, Dan?"

"No Jimmy, I have to go back inside and help the injured people."

"I'll go with you, Dan." he said, as he started to get up.

"No, Jimmy, you have to take care of your Mom."

"All right, Dan, but could you hurry up?" Jimmy had a look of sadness in his eyes.

Dan gave him a smile and a wink, "you betcha, partner."

Dan made his way back inside the car. As he looked around and scanned the situation, he saw that most of the seats had broken loose. Jagged strips of metal hung down like giant, grinning shark teeth. He wondered what genius, structural engineer, designed this hunk of twisted metal. Guess they thought it would never be involved in a crash...Dan jumped when someone's hand reached out and grasped Dan's ankle.

"Help me mister, help me!" It was that sweet old lady that was sitting behind him.

"Okay ma'am, take it easy," he replied as he lifted her carefully off the floor.

"Where's my husband?" she asked.

"Don't worry Ma'am," Dan answered her, as they made their way to the front of the car. "I'll come back and get him, after I get you outside, to safety, okay?" He led her to Sally and Jimmy. Then headed back into the train. Some passenger's where making their way out, through the front windshield, and that created a traffic jamb for him.

Dan finally made his way back into the car and started looking for the old lady's husband. He spotted him crumpled up on the floor, with a seat on top of his frail body. He reached down and checked for a pulse.

Nothing. He was as white as a ghost. Dan carefully lifted the chair of him and gently turned him on his back. Then he started CPR, hoping for the best. He firmly started pushing on his chest, several times. Nothing! All at once a large stream of blood and air gushed out of his mouth and nose. For a moment Dan thought the old fellow was going to make it. He continued the CPR for what seemed like an hour, but he just couldn't bring him back. Dan was sweating profusely and was fatigued. He looked up quickly, beginning to panic. He glanced around the car and shouted,

"Can someone give me a hand!"

"Sure buddy, what do you need!" a man called out. Dan spotted him halfway down the isle. He was staggering towards Dan. He looked a little groggy from the crash.

"What can I do to help?" He asked, reaching to help Dan.

"Could you take over the compressions for me?"

"Not a problem, pal, let me get in there." Dan slid out of the way and practically passed out. "You okay, buddy?"

"Yeah, just worn out, how's he doing?"

"Not good I don't think he's gonna make it."

Dan's eyes filled up with tears. He was super stressed out from all of this. And now he knew the old guy was dead.

"Are you alright?" the guy asked.

"I think so."

"Well you don't look good," he replied, then reached up, to shake Dan's hand, and added "My name in Hank Smith."

"Glad to meet you, Hank." Dan replied, reaching to shake Hank's hand, "I'm Dan Jensen, and I want to thank you for the help."

"Not a problem, Dan." Hank replied. Dan had a good vibe about this guy as soon as he shook his hand. He had a firm grip for a short, stocky guy. He also had a huge smile across his reddish face and a twinkle in his eye.

"What's your plan?" Hank asked.

"I haven't had time to think of one. What about you?"

"The way I see it," Hank started, "we need to evacuate this silver monster before anyone else dies." The analogy caught Dan's attention — wasn't that what Jimmy said?

"Let's start right over there," Hank suggested, and pointed to a injured lady against the wall. "We'll get her outside, then come back and work our way down the isle."

"Sounds good to me, but let's make sure we get the most severely wounded out first."

"Alright, that sounds good...plus we need to get somebody outside to nurse the wounded, and maybe get a fire started, to keep them warm. The sun is starting to set and it's going to get cold." Hank stated.

"Okay, let's get it done." Dan said. Hank shot him a smile and reached down to pick up the lady. They made it outside and carried the lady over to where he left Sally. Sally was grouped together, talking with about ten other people. Jimmy ran out of the group and yelled!

"Dan! Dan, over here!" He shouted, waving his arm's back and forth, through the air. "Over here."

Sally stood up and waved. She saw that they were carrying a injured lady. "Put her down over here Dan, we have some coats and a couple of blankets from the train." Hank and Dan made their way to the group.

"She's not too bad Sally, looks like a small cut on her back, but check her out totally, because we didn't have time to." Dan stated, as they laid her down on the makeshift bed. "Oh by the way, this is Hank Smith...Hank, this is Sally and Jimmy."

"Nice to meet you Hank...ah well...not in these circumstances, but you know what I mean."

"I do, Sally, and it's nice to meet you and, ah..." Hank stammered, and he got that lost look on his face. Jimmy jumped closer, held out his tiny hand.

"Jimmy, Jimmy Weeks!" He said, and started shaking

Hanks hand. Hank let go quickly,

"Ouch!" he shouted, teasingly, "That hurts!" And shook his hand in pain. Jimmy laughed, along with Dan and some others.

"We've got to get back in there, Sally, there's a lot more people in there that can't make it out on their own. "

"I understand Dan, no problem, go ahead, we'll be waiting for you. Oh, by the way, is your phone working? I tried calling my mother, and all I get is static."

"I'm not sure, let me see…" Dan tried calling his daughter…a lot of static, then a faint "hello daddy," followed by more static. Dan answered back,

"Jan…Jan! Can you hear me? Jan?"

"…da…y…"

"I can't get through Sally, we must be in a dead area, no phone service." With that said, Hank and Dan turned and started back towards the train.

"What about my husband?" a feeble voice asked, "You said that you were going for him."

Dan stopped dead in his tracks. That weird, dreadful feeling, went down the back of his neck again. He slowly turned to the fragile old lady.

"I'm sorry ma'am, but your husband didn't make it." She started shaking and weeping

"No, nooo, that can't be." Her legs gave out and she started to fall. Dan reached out and hugged her.

"I'm so sorry ma'am, we tried real hard to save him, but…" Dan tried to finish his statement, but he was to choked up to speak. Burning tears rolled down his face, he felt horrible for her. Second thoughts spread through his head, did he really do his best? Did he really tried his hardest? Or did he just give up to soon?

"Come on Dan," Hank said softly, "don't beat yourself up, you did everything that you could have possibly done."

Dan slowly sat the lady down and kissed her on her forehead. She looked up at him, her grey eyes loaded with tears,
that rolled down her wrinkled cheeks. Her frayed, tired, heart,
was broken for the very first time. Dan's stomach was killing
him. Hank held onto Dan's arm,

"Come on buddy, we've got go finish, what we started."

Dan was old school, he new just what Hank meant. It was
instilled in him since he was a boy. Everyday his father would
get him and his brother up at 5 a.m.. and tell them,

*Get out in the barn and get your chores done, then get back in
here for breakfast and don't be late for school.*"

He knew enough, not to talk back.

Hank and Dan made their way back into the "silver coffin."
There seamed to be more casualties than before. No wonder
Sally had called it a "silver tomb." Hank moved his stocky
frame through the wreck, with the agility of a cat. He lifted
debris off of people with ease. Dan was amazed, and knew
that Hank could get the job done.

"Okay Dan, let's get this guy out of here, he's bleeding
pretty bad..."

"You got it Hank." Dan said...In and out...over and over...
they transported the injured. It was getting dark now and
ghoulish shadows, hung over them, waiting for the moment
to make their strike. Hank lost count of all the injured that
him and Dan had moved out. Dan's back was killing him and
he had to stopped and stretch.

"I need to take a breather Hank, okay?"

"Sure thing buddy, I'll take this lady out and come back
in a second." Hank proceeded out and Dan sat down on a
broken seat. He looked around and heard a snap of electricity
streaking out from a wire. Then his eye caught a glimpse of
the ripped, sharp edges of the jagged steel, hanging down,
reaching for him. It made him shutter...He felt that It wanted

revenge; revenge from the "man" that ripped the soul out of the Silver Streak. It hungered for more death, …more blood… more souls…Dan looked up…he swore that a serrated metal shard, was just over his head, gleaming down at him, with the reflection of the fading sunlight. He swore it was grinning at him, daring him to come closer, so it could make a fatal slash on him or anyone else that dared come within it's reach…

"Dan…Earth to Dan! What the hell are you thinking about?" Dan snapped back into reality.

"What? Oh, nothing, just tired and my back is killing me."

"We're almost done buddy," Hank announced, "Just two or three more people are back in there, and then we got it made in the shade."

"You're not that old to remember that one, are you Hank?" Dan asked. "That's from the fifties."

"Yeah I know. My old man used to say that to me all the time, when I was growing up." They both laughed.

After everyone was out of the train and safe, Hank said he would go back in for a final check.

"No Hank, I'll do it. You're needed out here more then me. Get some fires going and try to settle everybody down. I'll make the last sweep."

"You got it, buddy," Hank agreed.

Dan made his way back in through the broken front windshield, bending down to make sure he didn't cut his back on the glass. It was very dark by now. He carefully walked back through the tangled mess, crunching glass under his feet with ever step. *"The moon must be coming out,"* he thought to himself. He reached for his cell phone and turned on the flash light app. He slowly walked to the rear of the car, feeling a little bit more secure, with his phone light illuminating the path.

Most of the dust and smoky gases had settled by now. Faint moonbeams cascaded through the broken window's above. The smell of smoldering wire's still lingered in the car. Dan's nerves where very rattled by now, not to mention his stress and fatigue.

Shadows grew long around him. A large dark shadow inched its way up his back and spread out over his shoulder's, then the back of his neck…He couldn't move, his head was spinning. He thought he was going to pass out. The cold, clammy, dampness, penetrated its death grip all the way to his spine. It seemed to take control of him.

Dan tried to turn around and face his imaginary enemy, but he couldn't move. He felt as through he was suspended in slow motion. He desperately tried to twist around and make an effort to grab it, whatever it was. Then as quickly as it came, it was gone. Or was it ever there?

"What the hell was that?" he said out loud. "I must be losing my fucking mind."

He continued on with his search. "Anybody here!?" He shouted. "Anybody left in here?" He hated doing this, but he felt obligated for some unknown reason. He tried to compose himself and settle his nerves, then he move onward.

A few more electrical spurts and sparks came alive over his head and fell down onto his arms and neck, stinging and burning his unprotected skin.

"That's it for me," he stated out loud, "I'm not going to fry in this murky tomb — screw this bullshit!" He was pissed off and tired, as he swept off the hot sparks that were burning him. He turned around and started to exit this hell hole.

"Mister…mister…help me…please…help me…" A frail, quivering voice begged him…again, that eerie feeling crept down the back of his neck. It was the same feeling you get when you speed past a state trooper with a radar gun. and you're doing thirty miles an hour over the limit.

"Mister…*help me*…"

Dan worked his way towards the failing voice. Moving a broken seat out of his pathway, he spotted her. He shined the phone light in her direction. She was sitting up against the wall and by the look on her face, she was in extreme pain. There was some blood on her blouse and hands.

"Can you move, ma'am?" Dan asked, as he looked at her. He thought she might be late forties, maybe fifty, very pale, It was hard to tell in this light.

"I don't think so...I hurt all over."

Dan bent down to comfort her. "I'm going to try to lift you up, and get you on your feet, alright?"

"I guess so..." He slowly placed his hands under her arm's, and then, gently began lifting her...

"Let me know if it hurts, okay?"

Just at that moment, that dark shadow engulfed him again. It was colder and darker than before. He quickly turned his head, to see what it was.

Nothing.

He turned back to the lady and realized that he was cheek to cheek with her now. He lifted her up a little more, then stopped. As he peered into her eyes, they seemed to get darker. Her face slowly began to alter...all of her veins and blood vessels became deep red and started to swell. Her face looked like a road map become flesh...her blood vessels continued to grow and started to burst under her pale skin, turning her entire face into pure blood. The skin on her arms started to crack and blood sprayed all over Dan's face and arms. Dan tried to scream— but nothing came out.

Her eyes bulged out of their sockets. One of her eyes shot out, like a missile and hit Dan square in his wide open mouth, the splattered like a broken egg yoke. The other flying eyeball hit him on his chest and rolled down the font of his shirt... He was gagging and choking but couldn't move. He tried to keep his eyes closed, but he instinctively looked at her again. Her eye sockets were pure black, deep, empty holes, with flesh colored veins and torn eye muscles, wiggling and dancing, as they reached out, searching for their warm, bloody, spheres of eye sight. Long grey maggots squirmed out of the beastly, rotting eye sockets. Dozens of them, wiggling and falling to the floor and then, slithering towards Dan as though, they had built-in radar.

Dan watched in total disbelief. He was quickly losing his sanity. He forced his eyes shut, making a grand effort to come back to reality. He wanted to scream and wake up from this cruel and horrific nightmare. He opened his eyes once again, his head was still spinning, and the nightmare was still in front of him. He pushed away from the decaying ghoul. He fell backwards, and gasped for air. He choked on the stench of her rotting flesh and toxic gases, mixed with the burning fumes, from the shredded electrical wires.

His brain couldn't comprehend any of this…he looked on in horror as her jaw bone, tore through her bloody skin. Her mouth opened so wide that her jaw snapped into pieces. A swarm of gnats gushed out of her mouth and hit Dan in the face. The rancid smell made Dan vomit all over himself and the floor. She began speaking, in a viper snake like voice:

"What do you think you're doing," she hissed, "you fucking bastard?"

Dan tried to cry out…nothing but a weak cough.

He tried to push himself away from her again. Her voice was not human; all he could hear was that terrifying hiss, and picture in his mind, a giant viper…

Dan realized that her twisted lips were not moving, what was left of them anyway. Then Dan felt something on his ankles. He looked down, the maggots had inched their way across the floor, to his shoes and now they were crawling on his ankles, and making their way up his legs!

"You stupid son of a bitch!" she hissed…"you're dead! You're all fucking dead!" She was laughing hysterically now! Dan totally collapsed and spread out on the floor. The maggots continued to crawl up his body…Somebody hollered from up front. He thought it might be Hank, and tried to holler back, but nothing came out.

"What's wrong sonny?" The old bitch hissed…"CAT GOT'CHR TONGUE?" She howled and laughed hysterically.

"DAN! What's wrong down there?" It was Hank, but he seemed a million miles away…

"…down here, Hank!" He choked out the words, and then started coughing. Dan heard the sound of Hank making his way down from the front of the car, crunching glass, banging metal, and throwing seats out of his way.

"You all right, buddy?"

"Let's get the hell out of here," he gagged.

"What about that lady?" Hank asked, pointing towards Monica.

"Are you kidding me?" Dan snapped back!

"What do you mean, Dan?

"Just look at her, she's a freak." Dan stated, as they both turned their cell phone lights on her. She was back to normal, just the way Dan first found her. Dan was freaking out again!

"Mister…" That frail voice spoke out again, "…mister, I see you got some help."

"That's right ma'am and we'll get you out of here in a jiffy." Hank stated.

Dan didn't know what hell was going on, but he wasn't about to touch that witch. Hank leaned over and started to lift her up.

"Be careful, my arm hurts…I think it's cut. By the way, my name is Monica and you're Hank, right?"

"That's right, and I'll go easy, Monica, just let me know if I'm hurting you." She smiled at Hank and then gave Dan a evil grin. She started chatting with Hank like they were old friends.

"I was asking for help before, you know, right after the crash, but everyone just passed me by…" She explained to Hank. "I was getting real worried, I thought I would die back here." She continued, "Then that other fella showed up, you know, your buddy over there, and he didn't seem to care either…so I'm glad you came along." she said with a grin, looking over at Dan.

"Don't you worry, Monica. We're almost out of here," Hank reassured her. When Hank got Monica safely outside he told her it was a pleasure to meet her.

"Pleasure is all mine, Hank." she said with a grin. Dan couldn't believe it. If Hank only saw what I saw, he would've left her back there to die. Dan didn't know what this bitch was up to…But he sure as hell would find out.

Dan hesitated and took one final scan of the dark tomb. He still didn't understand what had just happened, or what he saw, but he didn't have time to figure it out. He just wanted to get the hell out of dodge.

Dan bent down and ducked under the jagged windshield, he made his final exit from this hell hole. When he got outside, he stood up and stretched his throbbing back, drew in a big breath of fresh air, and exhaled it slowly. It was the best smell; he could smell the pine trees, the sweet smell of honey suckle, and other wild flowers, and the aroma of the camp fire smoke, swirling through the trees and the wrecked train. Dan drew in a few more deep breaths and wandered over to the camp fire.

Jimmy greeted him with a hug and told him how much he had missed him. Sally gave him a warm smile and held her hand out for him to come over. Dan joined the group and the chatter continued flowing…

"You look exhausted, Dan." Sally said, looking at the stress in his eyes.

"Yeah, it's been a long day."

"You want something to eat, Dan?" Jimmy asked, holding up an over-stuffed bag.

"Sure, partner," Dan answered, "I'm starving, what do you got?"

"Well, some guys raided the food storage cabinets on the train, so I've got a good selection of stuff, and lots of it." Jimmy stated, as he dug into his bag, and produced a couple packs of goodies. They found a nice spot to sit down by the fire and took a well deserved rest. Dan chatted with Jimmy and Sally for quite some time before he started to doze off. He caught himself every now and then, but he tried to stay awake.

"Okay Jimmy, time to say goodnight to Dan." Sally ordered.

"Come on Mom, just a little longer?"

"I don't think so, young man. You and I will be right over there," she said, nodding towards a pile of coats and some blankets, "you can see Dan from there, and he will join us soon." she said, looking at Dan, "won't you?"

"Ahh, I guess I will…"

They headed for their new sleeping quarters. Jimmy was holding Sally's hand and complaining and looking back at Dan.

"But mom I don't have any school tomorrow, why do I have to go to bed so soon?"

"Because Jimmy, just because." Dan laughed at that. All mothers are alike.

Dan stared at the flames from the fire. They brought him back to a time when he was a Boy Scout. Good memories he thought. The younger guys, the ones wearing the NFL jerseys, were tending the fire with plenty of branches and logs. The camp fire was good-sized, and really warm, just what Dan needed…now if he only had some whiskey for the pain. He tried calling his daughter again…no luck.

People were moaning and groaning, cackling like old crows, sitting on a telephone wire…yak…yak…yak…it was starting to get on Dan's nerves.

"They should be grateful that they are alive." a voice stated behind him. Dan didn't recognize the voice. He looked around him to see where it came from. The young guy that busted out the windshield, was grinning at him. Dan stood up and headed for Jimmy and Sally before he said something that he would regret, and get himself into trouble. He settled down next to Jimmy, who was already out like a light, he rolled onto his back and closed his eyes…

"Good night, Dan." Sally whispered.

Without looking over at her, Dan whispered back "Good night Sally." He drifted off to sleep, and slept like a baby.

Until the nightmares started.

He saw the train crashing and Phil's chest being punctured by the tree limb, then Monica's beastly face and giant maggots chewing on his legs.

Dan jumped from his sleep, he forget where he was. As he sat up, his eyes still closed, he automatically raised his hands up, and rubbed the sleep out of them. A sharp pain flew up his back and that got his attention, real fast! As he looked around the makeshift campsite, it all came back to him instantly.

"About time you woke up, sleepy." Hank said with a grin, "How ya feeling?"

"Like I got run over by a train." he said, "I ache all over, especially my back. And I have a chill too, from the damp ground. I sure could use a cup of hot coffee."

"I guess I could help you out with that, partner." Hank stated. "A couple of guys went back into the train this morning, and found some more supplies." Then he held out a plastic cup, steaming with hot coffee.

"Thanks Hank, I sure do appreciate it," Dan reached out for the cup and took a sip. "Ahhh, not bad, Hank…not bad at all…by the way, how in the hell, are they making the coffee?"

"You wouldn't believe me if I told you…they found some used cans and bottled water…then…"

"Forget it Hank, I don't wanna know."

They both laughed out loud.

"Hey, you got any Tylenol, or anything for pain? My back is killing me."

"Looks like it might rain," Hank stated, "we better find some shelter, and no, I don't have any Tylenol" He laughed. Out in the distance, Dan thought he saw something, maybe a hunting cabin, it was hard to tell, through the scattered fog…

"You see that, over there Hank?" Dan asked, pointing in the direction of the structure.

"Yeah…" Hank replied, squinting, in that direction, "Might be a small barn or a 'lean-to'…"

"You're probably right, my eye's aren't as good as they used to be." Dan stated, "At any rate, I think we should check it out, could be a good place to hold up, if the weather turns bad."

"Sounds good to me, let's have another cup of joe and then we will head over there." Hank took the cups over to the young guys and returned with two full ones.

Dan smiled and took his coffee, they both sat down. Hank remembered the first time that he was in a "lean-too." He was around eight years old or so. His older brother, Jackie and his friend, Bobby, built one out of sugar maple trees, rope and the boughs of pine trees.

"Hank, let's take a walk over there and see what that shadow is." Dan stated, pointing at the structure.

"Sounds good to me Dan, let's go." He replied. They started out, when Jimmy hollered:

"Hey Dan, where you guys going?"

Before they could answer him, he asked, "Can I go with you?"

Dan looked over at Sally. She smiled and gave Dan a thumbs-up.

"Sure Jimmy," Dan answered, "Let's go," and away they went... *The Three Musketeers.*

It took them about ten minutes to reach their destination. The morning mist was burning off and the sun was starting to shine.

"Well, it's definitely a Lean-to Shelter, and a large one, at that." Hank confirmed. They checked it out, while Jimmy was running around and trying to get them to play tag.

"Looks like it's good shape," Hank stated, as he continued his inspection.

"Yeah, looks pretty good." Dan acknowledged. "Looks like we could set up a base camp here, stock up what little supplies we have and get two or three fires going."

"Sounds good. Maybe we could make a plan to get some help?" Hank questioned.

"What about playing tag?" Jimmy asked?

"A little later on, pal..." Dan stated and then suggested, "Let's head back and give everybody the news."

They went back, had something to eat, and then Dan made the announcement.

"Good morning everybody..." nobody paid attention to him, there was thirty to forty people in this group and there was three other groups close by from the other car, and most of them were chatting and ranting about one thing or another.

Hank let out old-fashion whistle! Then he shot his hands up in the air and waved them frantically.

"LISTEN UP PEOPLE! Dan has something to say!" They brought it down a few notches, but still kept muttering among themselves.

"We've found a large, 'lean-to' type shelter over there." Dan stated, pointing towards it. "We can set up a temporary home base where we store blankets, food and other supplies. We can also make space for the wounded."

"Who died, and left you boss?" some loud mouth yelled out, "You're not in charge"

There was a mixed response from the crowd, some of them clapped, and others booed.

"Give him a chance to talk, I want to hear what he's got to say" somebody else yelled out.

"Yeah, me too…I want to hear him!"

Then the first guy shot back "This is bull-shit, I'll bet somebody will be here to rescue us, any time now!" Everyone started getting upset, and most of them, looked confused.

"Please, just hear me out," Dan proclaimed, as he continued to relay his ideas and plans. The loud mouth and two or three other guys, threw up their hands, made some quip remarks and walked away. Some of the others moved up closer and listen intently. After Dan completed his speech, the group began gathering their supplies and belongings. They walked over to their new base and began distributing their luggage, supplies and what little food they had left into the shelter.

"Hey Dan, we're running low on food and water." a sweet, middled age woman stated. Dan turned and looked at her.

"Ah, hello," he said. She grabbed Dan's hand and shook it.

"My name is Hellen Higgins. I'm a retired school teacher." she stated, and before Dan could say another word, she continued, "how are we going to feed these folks, and make sure they have enough water?" She seemed a little flustered.

"Okay Hellen, calm down, we will come up with a plan." Dan reassured her, "By the way, did you meet everyone?"

"I've met Sally and Jimmy…oh and Bernice, she's right over there." Dan looked over and saw the old lady, whose husband had died in the crash. "She asked me to make her some tea, do we have any?"

"I'm not sure, that's Sally's department. By the way Hellen, this is Hank."

"Hi Hellen, nice to meet you, maybe we could find an old pot or a small bucket that we could boil some water in for tea." Hank suggested. She smiled at Hank.

"That would be nice."

"And we could check the coffee supplies for some tea bags." Hank offered.

"That sounds like a good idea, Hank." Hellen stated, and walked over to Bernie, to give her the good news about finding her some tea. Hank walked over to Jimmy and asked him if he wanted to go for a walk?

"Where to, Hank?"

"Exploring buddy."

"Exploring for what?" Jimmy shot back...

"Exploring for supplies and food. Who knows what we might find?"

"That sounds cool, Hank, when do we get started?"

"Right now pal."

Jimmy jumped for joy, and took off like a rocket.

"That kid is full of piss and vinegar, isn't he Dan?"

"You got that right Hank, and you better hurry up 'cause he's almost out of sight!" Hank turned around to look.

"Yo, slow down buddy, wait for me!" Hank started to sprint after him, but after a few yards, he had to slow down to a jog.

After an hour or so, Hank and Jimmy returned with their hands full of junk. At least it looked that way to Sally. She walked over to Dan and motioned for him to look at Jimmy, then she shouted out to Jimmy,

"What do you have there, sweetie?" She asked, with a grin,

"Mom, Mom, you won't believe all the stuff we've found, real neat things too, show her Hank, show her!" Jimmy proudly exclaimed, holding out his "stuff" for her to look at. Hank unloaded his bounty and began to divided it up on the ground.

"Here you go Hellen," Hank proudly stated, handing her an old pewter pot, "It's a little dirty, but I check it for leaks and it seems to be in good condition. It might take a little elbow grease to get it clean, but it should do the job.

"Hey Dan, we also found a spring, just over that knoll" Jimmy reported.

"And there's plenty of dried, seasoned wood over their too, for our campfires," Hank added, with a large smile on his face.

"Man, you two guys, must of have been busy bees all day long over there." Dan said smiling. "I'll see if I can round up some help and they could give a hand to help gather some firewood. On second thought, I'll put Sally in charge of the firewood detail. That will give us time to make plans for a search party — alright Hank?"

"That's a good idea Dan, because I don't see anybody, breaking any speed records to find us. It's like we don't even exist. And by the way, Dan, you noticed something else?"

"What's that?"

"Nobody's phones are ringing anymore."

"I know, strange, isn't it?" Dan answered.

Dan kept thinking about the strange situation that they were all thrown into. First the crash, then the horrible deal in the back of the train with Monica, then the animosity with that guy last night and all the weird feelings he had been getting lately...

Everybody pitched in and lent a helping hand, even some of the wounded helped out. Bernice got her hot tea and a couple of cookies, while Hellen chatted with her. Sally and her crew were just returning from gathering the fire wood. Even Jimmy had his arms full small pine logs. By the time Dan and Hank wrapped up their private meeting, the group had two fires started and burning nicely.

"Is this one too big for the fire, Dan?" Jimmy asked, dragging over a large limb.

"No, not at all," he replied, "the bigger the better, pal." Jimmy was dirty from head to toe, but he was having the time of his life.

"This is just like camping out, right Dan?"

"You got that right buddy. Now all we need is some grub."

"What's grub Dan?" Jimmy asked.

"You know, food, hot dogs, hamburgers, baked beans. Maybe even some rabbit stew, if we could trap one."

"Rabbit stew? Are you kidding me? Yuck! I couldn't eat that," Jimmy said as he held his hand over his mouth, pretending to gag.

"What about baked beans?" Hank chimed in.

"I don't like them either." Jimmy answered.

"Beans have lots of protein, and you need protein to stay fit, especially out here in the wilderness pal." Dan stated, holding back a laugh.

"And you know the old saying, about beans, don't ya Jimmy?" Hank asked.

"No, what' that?"

"Beans, beans, good for your heart. The more you eat, the more you fart!"

Everybody burst into laughter. Jimmy almost fell on the ground, laughing so hard. It was good to see smiles on their faces, and get their minds off of their horrendous situation that they had no control over.

It does feel good to be out here, Dan thought, wherever out here was. He looked up at the sky. It was a clear night, a bit on the cool side, but not cold. The camp fires were crackling and popping. The smell of burning pine wood was drifting through the still air. The red and yellow flames were licking the pine logs into submission, surrendering their solid form into glowing embers, then ashes and smoke. It was almost hypnotic, staring into that welcoming inferno. Dan's thoughts grew deep. The fire made him feel secure. It brought back the cherished memories of his childhood: camping out in the woods with his scout pack, roasting hot dogs and marshmallows into the wee hours of the night. And of coarse, the ghost stories…

Patti and Jerry kept to themselves most of the day. As they sat on the far side of the fire pit, she was explaining to him about the nightmares that she was having about their father. She hated thinking about it, let alone talking about it, but Jerry was a good listener and she loved her brother dearly.

"Don't worry sis, we're free now and the past will fade away eventually. We will get out of this mess and start our lives over again, and they will never find us. I promise you."

People started gathering now, drawn to the warmth of the fire. Dan stood up and decided to take a head count. He mumbled, while he counted,

"hmm, twenty, …mmm, …maybe twenty five, maybe thirty…" It was hard get a accurate total, because they kept moving, here and there, forming small groups and then some would shift to another group…

Two more camp fires sprung up, about a hundred yards away, with maybe fifteen or so people gathering around them. Dan couldn't recognize anybody in the other groups, they were too far away for his old eyes.

"Let's sit down and take a load off." Hank suggested, to everybody. Dan snapped out of his thoughts.

"Sounds like a good idea," Hellen stated. They all sat down, Hellen covered Bernice with a blanket and then sat next to her and gave her a hug. "Does that feel better Bernice?"

"Oh my, yes it does. But you don't have call me Bernice, just call me Bernie, all my friends call Bernie," she said, with a big smile. Everyone smiled at that, while looking at Bernie. That made Dan feel good and he looked at Sally and smiled. Jimmy had his head in her lap and his eye's were starting to close. Dan whispered to Sally, ..." He looks pooped." "Yeah... it's been a long, hard day," she whispered back,

"How is your back feeling?"

"Ahh, it's okay, I guess. Hank gave me a couple sampler bottles of scotch from the train, and that took the edge off." Dan answered, with a slight grin. Sally smiled at him and he smiled back and gave her a wink. After a short while, they both started to drift off.

Dan started thinking about the meeting he had this morning with Hank...

"So what's are next move Dan?"

"I'm not sure. Maybe split up into two groups? Then follow the train tracks in both directions and look for the first town or village that we come across. I don't know, what do ya think Hank?"

"Sounds like a good idea to me, what about a third group going on the dirt road that Jimmy and I found when we were searching for supplies this morning? I saw that it was going eastward. That might be worth a look, what do you think?"

"Alright, that's as good as any place to look for help." Dan responded. "So first thing in the morning, right after breakfast, we'll gather everybody together and have a big meeting."

"Sounds good, do you think we should invite the 'loud mouth' and his group?"

"Yeah. We're going to need all the help we can get." Dan answered.

"I guess you're right, buddy."

DAY THREE

Hank got up at the crack of dawn. The embers were still glowing in the fire pit. He gathered up some twigs and pine needles and threw them on the hot embers and it instantly burst into flames. It crackled and popped as Hank fed it small limbs and branches. He filled the pewter pot with water for coffee and tea and set it on a make-shift grill, and soon it was boiling.

Dan stirred and peeked over at Jimmy, he was still asleep. Hank spotted Dan.

"Up and at 'em, do you think you're gonna sleep all day?"

"Very funny…bud." Dan stated. Sally wiggled Jimmy and he started to moan.

"Time to get up sweetie."

"Oh Mom, do I have to?"

"You bet you do." Dan chimed in. "We've got a lot of things to do today pal"

"Alright, I'll get up."

About a hour later, everyone was finishing their breakfast. While they were cleaning up the area, Dan was thinking about what he would say at the meeting. His mind started to wander. Where are we? What state are we in? What exactly happened? Why did we crash? Where did the tracks go? Why did they end, with out a warning? No signs, no yellow caution tape… nothing. All Dan could remember was that he was drifting off when all hell broke loose. After a few moments he snapped back to the present and looked around.

"Are you folks ready to get started with the meeting?" Dan asked.

"Yeah, sure, sounds good to us." one answered. Some nodded their heads, some didn't seem interested at all.

"Alright, before we get started with meeting, Hank had a

good suggestion, that we should have small meeting first so we can get our idea's down and then call everybody together for the main meeting. And I also he thought we could have someone take notes."

"I could take the notes," Hellen announced, "I used to be a teacher."

"That would be fine, Hellen," Dan stated, "and thank you so much for helping with everything." Hellen started to blush, "You're welcome, I'm just doing my fair share."

"Okay let's get started." Dan stated. "I'm not too sure what happened because I was nodding off. How about you Hank, do you know what happened?"

"Nope, I feel asleep." Hank answered, "Me too," Hellen stated, "How about you, Sally? Do you recall anything?"

"No. Jimmy and I both fell asleep. Don't remember anything."

"Does anybody remember what happened?" Hank asked, looking around for a answer. Same story from all of them. Sleeping.

"Excuse me sir, my name is, Joe Rodgers, the one you saved on the train" Dan shook his and said, "Glad to meet Joe, I don't recall saving you, but there was a lot going on yesterday."

"There sure was, Dan, but you did save me and by the way I was also fast asleep when the train crashed. But I have a theory about the this whole thing. Wanna hear it?"

Dan looked at Joe, he looked alright, average size, a little chunky, he didn't look like a nut. He was sweating profusely, red in the face and squinted as he talked. Dan wasn't sure of what he was going to say...

"Ah, I guess so..." Dan answered, not sure of how this was going to go. "Will this take a long time to explain, Joe?" Dan asked.

"Not at all guys," Joe answered with a smile. "First of all I'd like to say hello to everyone." People smiled and nodded their heads, some gave a brief wave. "Now the way I figure, everybody here was sleeping, right?"

Everyone acknowledged him and agreed.

"The question is, where and when did you fall asleep?"

There was puzzled looks all around and some whispers to each other. No doubt trying to figure out where they fell asleep.

"Now I'm pretty sure that I fell asleep right after that stop in Pennsylvania, you know, um…that little city, ah…what was it called?"

"Scranton!" someone hollered out.

"Oh yeah, that's it. Well, anyway, that's the last thing I remember. The train got rolling, and I drifted off…"

"That sounds just about the way I recalled it, too." Sally affirmed.

"Me too!" piped in Jimmy. Everyone looked lost in thought.

"I fell asleep before that, I don't even remember stopping in P.A." Dan said.

"Now, I'm no genius and don't know anything about physics," Joe continued, "But if some of us fell asleep somewhere in central PA, and, the next thing we know, we wake up to a horrible train wreck, right here," Joe said, looking around…"Ah…I'm not exactly sure, where 'here' is…but it sure isn't Pennsylvania or even Ohio."

Now everybody looked upset and very confused, including Dan and Hank.

"So, just what are you saying, Joe?" Dan asked. "What's your theory?"

"Yeah, what is your theory Joe?" Hank cut in, "What are you trying to explain?"

"I'm not really sure, but I'm thinking we are out west somewhere, maybe close to a desert or maybe the badlands. Hell, I'm not sure, but it's all crazy. But I know one thing, we gotta find some real food, and get some help for the injured folks, and get back home, where we belong."

Everyone nodded their heads in agreement.

"That sounds good Joe," Dan stated, "Now let's get all the people together and start the meeting."

"Sounds good Dan," Hank responded, "and I'll go get those other groups, to join us." Hank took off and rounded up the other groups. By the time he got back, it was well after lunch.

THE MEETING

Everybody was slowly gathering around — some were standing but most were sitting. The noise level was up, as Hank and Dan tried to gain some control of the situation. A few of the younger kids were running around playing tag and having a good time.

"PEOPLE !" Dan shouted ! "Could you please quiet down and take a seat?"

A hush swept over the crowd, more people sat down and other's were shushing their neighbors.

"Please, quiet down," Dan expressed again. Hank was taking a head count for Dan and feeding the info to Hellen, for the record.

"Thank your time and patience." Dan announced, "I'd like to start off by introducing myself and a few others. My name is Dan Jensen, this is Hank Smith," he stated as he gestured for Hank to stand, "This is Sally Weeks,"

Before Dan could get another word out, someone yelled, "Come on, let's go, I got stuff to do!" This brought some laughter and chuckles out of the crow.

"Alright," Dan thought, "there's always an ass-hole in the bunch." Hank started getting a little pissed. He looked like he was getting ready to kick some ass. Sally and Hellen looked worried.

"Alright," Dan tried again, "I'll get right to the point! We need to form a search party, and go find some help." Most of people looked interested in what Dan was saying. "We have three directions to go in," Dan began, explaining the plan that Hank and the others came up with.

"So, can I get some volunteers?" he asked. Just then a verbal fight broke out in the back of the crowd.

"Screw you asshole!" a short, fat guy yelled

"NO, fuck you asshole!" a large man shouted louder. The short guy looked intimidated.

"I am going with them!" he raged, pointing in Dan's direction, "I like their ideas and I like the way that they thought this whole plan through..."

"Well your not taking my flashlight with you!" The larger man commanded, as he grabbed the base of the flashlight.

The short guy pulled back, and shouted, "It's not even your flashlight!"

He cried out as the big guy started twisting it out of his hands, "you found it in the emergency box, so that makes it everybody's!" The big guy won the tug-of-war and the little guy slipped and fell backwards, hitting the ground hard.

"Whoa!, take it easy! Your scaring the little kids and we don't need that profanity either!" Dan shouted, as he watched Hank make his way over to the two troublemakers.

"Now what seems to be the problem?" Hank sternly asked. He noticed the short guy was getting up off the ground. "Oh... it's you Joe, What the hell is going on?

"I'll tell ya, what's going on, he's trying to take the flashlight from me."

"Screw that, I'll tell you what the real problem is! It's this short, little prick," He yelled and tried to pushed Joe backwards.

"Knock it off," Hank warned, "what's your name anyway?"

"What's it to ya?" He snapped back.

Hank was getting really pissed. He wanted to punch the guy in the face. He decided to be diplomatic, and diffuse the situation. "Listen guy, we're just trying to get organized, get everybody on the same page, do ya know what I mean?"

"…yeah, I guess so. Sorry I lost my cool." He sincerely replied, "My name is Pete Perry, from New York City."

"Nice to meet you Pete. Sorry it isn't under better circumstances." Hank replied. Dan made his way over to them, and Hank introduced them.

"So what do you think about the plan, Pete?" Dan asked.

"It's okay, but I've got my own plans." he stated.

"And what are they" Hank piped in, "if you don't mind me asking."

"I don't mind at all." Pete shot back, "I'm going back the way we came from. That's the logical thing to do."

"And why's that Pete?" Hank asked quickly.

"Because I'm a leader, not a follower. I'm the 'can-do-man,' and by God, that's what I'm gonna do, so who's with me? Anybody?"

A couple guys yelled out, "you got it…sounds good, yep, sounds good…"

Hank was thinking, "*who died and left this asshole in charge?*"

"Listen, Pete, I'm not running the show or anything, I just don't want to see everybody going in different directions. We don't even know where we are, and it's getting dark." Dan stated, almost apologetic, "so how about we sit down and look over the plans, and coordinate things, so no one gets hurt, or lost? Make sense?"

"Well, Dan, you do it your way and I'll do it mine, and we'll see who comes up on top." Dan didn't know what to say at this point. Hank kept his mouth shut, because he knew if he started, shit was going to happen, and besides that, he hoped this asshole would get lost and never find his way back.

Pete's face was turning red, and his breathing was labored. Dan was thinking it was a stroke or a heart attack…this guy doesn't have a chance.

"Who's with me!" Pete announced, "anybody want to get the hell out of here, and back to civilization? Follow me if you do." He was hell bent on leaving. Two guys stood up and walk away with him.

"Could be trouble." A man's voice stated behind Dan. He turned around to see who It was…he didn't recognize the guy. He was very large and tall, with rugged features, he reminded Dan of mob guy. Dan didn't remember seeing him on the train…but he didn't give it much thought, there was a lot going on in the wreck, and who knew how many faces he might have missed…

"Let me introduce myself — Dave Cummings," he offered, extending his large hand to Dan. He firmly gripped Dan's hand. It felt cool to the touch, even cold, as they shook hands. His large hand felt like a baseball glove, making Dan feel insecure for a second. His grip seemed to tighten, he was very strong and that's the message he wanted to convey to Dan. He looked Dan straight in the eyes and gave Dan a deceiving grin. He kept a secure grip on Dan's hand and Dan tried to return the energy. Dan didn't like this guy, at all.

"Dan is the name. Dan Jensen. Nice to meet you Dave," he lied.

"Looks like you've got a problem here," Dave stated, looking over at Hank.

"They're just getting aggravated, that's all." Dan replied.

"Well I say, if they want out, let them go, they'll be back." With that said, Dave walked away from Dan and the others, and looked at Hank again.

"What the hell was that all about?" Hank asked, as the others looked at Dan.

"The hell if I know." Dan commented, and then asked Hank, "and how does he know that they will be back?"

"That guy is very strange." Sally stated.

"Yeah," Joe added, "I saw him about two hours ago, I don't know where he came from, and I don't remember him from the train, either."

"This doesn't add up Hank, not at all," Dan mumbled.

"Speaking of adding up, Dan — I've got a total for you, on the head count."

"Go 'head, what do you got?" Hank walked over to Hellen and got the notes.

"Well to begin with, I got a total of 47 people. And that's counting the injured."

"We had more then that in our car alone." Dan shot back, "and what about the deceased? There had to be, five or six of them, right?"

"That's what I thought too, but I did get a chance to go over and check, oh, and another thing," Hank paused, "I met some people on the train when we started out in New York and I don't see them now. Where the hell did they go? I know they didn't die in the crash or we would have carried them out."

"Come to think Hank, I remember some other people too, and I don't see them." Dan pondered, "so what the hell is going on here...I just don't get it..."

"Stop you two," Sally softly demanded, "Your scaring Jimmy and me as well."

"Where do you think the rest are, Dan?" Hellen inquired?

"Yeah Dan." Joe chimed in. Dan saw that Sally was really getting upset.

"Okay, let's take a breath, let's not get nutty now. Just think it through." Dan offered." Just then Dan felt a cold shiver rundown his spine, He loathed this feeling. He immediately got stomach cramps. Holding his stomach, he looked up to see if anyone noticed. That's when he spotted Dave Cummings talking with Pete Parry.

Placing his hand on Pete's shoulder, he continued his conversation, like they were old college buddies. Dave glanced over at Dan, and gave a quick smirk.

"I definitely don't like that guy." He said under his breath.

"What's that Dan?" Hank quietly asked.

"Nothing, nothing at all…"

Pete and a small group of guys said their good byes, shook hands with Dave Cummings and asked one more time if anyone would like to join them.

As they turned to leave, Pete held up the flashlight, and let out a shrilling whistle and yelled:

"HEY JOEY, I've got your flashlight!" He stated laughing along with the guys in his group.

At the last second, Joey jumped up and shouted:

"Hey, wait a second!" He started to run towards Pete's group. "Wait up! I'm going with you guys!" He was running as fast as he could. Hank and Dan were in disbelief.

"What? Where the hell is he going?" Dan yelled out.

"Beats the shit out me." Hank said.

When Joe reached Pete and the others, he quickly got into a conversation with them. Pete handed over the flashlight and patted Joe on the back and gave him a big smile. Then they all turned and walk away into the nights darkness.

Dan and the rest watched, as their backs disappeared into the dark night. Two of them were carrying makeshift torches, that might last an hour or two. As they traveled farther and farther away, the flare from the torches was all anyone could see, shimmering in the night.

Finally, all anyone could see were two 'cat's eyes' from the glowing torches in the darkness, until they too, disappeared into the black abyss…

Things got quiet for awhile. Sally put Jimmy down to sleep. Dan and Hank started gearing up for their trip. Hellen comforted Bernice and tucked her into bed. Patti and Jerry Cooper threw a few more logs on the fire and talk quietly to each other.

"We had better get started Dan." Hank stated. Dan was regretting this journey already. It hadn't even started yet, but he had bad vibes.

"You're right Hank. It's time to roll. We better get someone to replace Joe, don't ya think?"

"Yeah, that sounds like a good idea. I'll ask around."

Hank came back a few minutes later with a guy named Eli Washington. He had rugged features and a muscular build. Hank thought he looked ex-military. He would definitely be an asset for them.

"Come on over Eli, meet the guys" Hank made the introductions to all. They all seemed to warm up to Eli immediately, he looked very secure and confident. Patti thought he looked just like Denzel.

"Are you ready to go guys?" Dan asked.

"Yeah Dan," they nodded their heads, adjusted their backpacks and checked their water supply.

Jerry snickered at the thought of all his extra money that he had in his wallet and sneakers. It was ironic, he thought, all that money and no place to spend it. Patti looked at him and wondered what he was smiling at. Hank checked the flashlight on his phone. Dan checked his.

"Everybody ready?" Dan asked again.

"Alright, let's get started."

After a few hugs and kisses, they started out. Jimmy finally dozed off. His tender head laying softly on his mothers lap, as she gently stroked his golden hair.

The camp fire crackled and emitted orange, red, and blue-green flames. Jimmy woke up from a bad dream, and was leaning against his mom, and she was leaning against one of the support posts of the Lean-To. He stared at the soothing flames, and thought about how much he missed Dan. He really wasn't missing his father, and he couldn't understand why that was. Thethought disappeared as fast as it came. Directly across from him, Hellen and Bernie were sitting, getting nice and warm from the inviting fire. They noticed a nice young woman tending the fire.

"Hellen, do you know that young lady over there, by the fire?" Bernie asked.

"I don't believe so…but she seems quite nice. Want me to go over and say hi?"

"That you be nice." Bernie replied. So Hellen got up and walked over…

"Hello there — my name is Hellen Higgins."

Jackie looked up, and gave Hellen a big smile, and tossed the remaining two logs on the fire, causing the burning embers to shoot sparks into the night. They both jumped back a step, and laughed.

"Sorry about that." Jackie said with a giggle, "My name is Jackie Lombardo, and it's nice to meet you, Hellen." They chatted for a minute or two, then Hellen invited her to go over and meet the girls.

"Jackie, I would like to meet Bernie, the school teacher," she said with a grin.

"Oh stop it," Bernie said jokingly, "Hellen is the school teacher, not me. She just loves to kid around. It's very nice to meet you Jackie." Sally and Jimmy walked over and Hellen introduced them to Jackie also. They all sat next to the warm fire and talked the night away.

"So Hellen," Jackie inquired, "tell me how it was to be a grade school teacher?"

"Oh my goodness, I don't want to bore everyone again with my life story."

"Come on, we want to hear it again." everybody cheered in, giggling.

"Alright, you asked for it," Hellen shot back, with a smile on her blushing cheeks.

"It all started a while ago…" she started. She then recounted her many adventures, before interrupting herself.

"I was quite fortunate to have the means to travel the world during my summer breaks. My husband had a very successful business." Hellen stated, "But I have to admit, of all my exciting trips around the world, I believe this one is going to be the most exciting trip I have ever embarked on. We will remember it forever."

That statement seemed a strange to Bernie and Sally. The rest of the group were nodding their heads in agreement, confirming what Hellen had just said. They had no way of knowing that they were, as Hellen said, starting upon the journey of a lifetime.

By the time Hellen had finished her story, many other people had joined the assemblage of her new admirers. A few standing but most sitting, glued to the fire and her storie.

A guy named John Collins introduced himself to Hellen and Bernie. He sat down beside them and told Hellen how much he had enjoyed her stories.

"Thank you John! That's very nice of you to say." Hellen said. "John, I'm going to tuck Bernie in for the night, and when she dozes off, would you like to continue are conversation?"

"Sure, sounds good to me." He answered, with a polite smile. Hellen smiled back and noticed that John was quite attractive, she blushed at that thought. He had wavy brown hair, a big smile, muscular build, and hazel eyes…

After she got Bernie all tucked in, she leaned over and gave her a good night kiss on her forehead.

"Good night sweet heart."

"And good night to you too, Hellen," Bernie said giddily.

"Don't be up to late with your new beau,"

"Oh stop that Bernie, he's just being nice."

"Sure he is, that's why your flirting with him."

"I'm not flirting," Hellen said, while blushing. "I'm just trying to be polite."

"Sure you are."

John and Hellen talked into the wee hours of the night. Mostly small talk about their lives and future dreams. He told her that he was a golf pro up until five years ago, when he had to retire due to a back operation.

"Retired? You're too young to be retired."

"What do you mean, "too young?" I'm forty five and I fell like sixty." They both laughed at that one. They were getting along just fine. Then the conversation turned a little more serious.

"So I was planning to take a group of people over where Hank and Jimmy found that dirt road. Maybe we can find some help down that way."

"I guess it makes sense," Hellen said, "but so many have gone searching already, you know: Dan, Hank, and that other group. I'm just worried, I guess."

"I can relate to that, I know how you feel," John replied, "but I just have this gut feeling…like I've gotta do something to help."

"Let's talk about it in the morning, OK?" Hellen suggested. John nodded in agreement, and stood up, smiled and walked over to the fire. He tossed a few more logs on it, waved good night to Hellen, then walked across to the lean-to, laid down and went to sleep.

The sun was warm and bright the next morning. Sally was rationing out the remainder of food that was semi-nutritious. The rest was all junk food: candy bars, pretzels, chips, and few cup cakes. Jimmy was playing with two other kids that were about his age. Hellen was tending to Bernie. The new guy, John, was trying to scrounge up some volunteers for the search party, and not having much luck. After a while, he walked over to Hellen.

"How's it going John?"

"Not too good. I got one 'maybe,' and ten 'no's.' And the rest of them I didn't ask because they had some injuries."

"Well, they are pretty worn out and exhausted," Bernie added, "but I'm sure you'll find someone to join you." She didn't sound very convincing, but it was the thought that counted.

"Yeah, John, I agree with Bernie, you'll find someone. Now let's go over and see Sally before all the good stuff is gone." They walked over and said good morning.

"Morning all..." Sally offered, "How was your night?"

"Not too bad sweetie," Bernie answered as she accepted her breakfast protein bar.

"I slept like a log." John offered. "Me too." Hellen chimed in. Bernie giggled under her breath. They all sat down and slowly ate their food. Jimmy ran over and grabbed whatever Sally had to offer, devoured it, and took off to play again. He turned quickly and shouted back to John.

"Hey John! I forgot to tell ya. Some lady told me to tell ya she'll go with you to search for help!"

"Send her over! I can use all the help I can get." After they finished eating, they helped Sally clean up. Sally was just about to ask them what their plans were for the day.

"Hi, I'm Monica. Little Jimmy said that you were looking for volunteers."

"You bet," John replied. "I'm John Collins, nice to meet you, Monica."

"John Collins, that sounds like a mixed drink." She said, amused, and with a wide pleasant smile. Hellen instantly took note of that.

"Well it's nice to meet you to, Monica," John said reaching out to shake her hand. "So you wouldn't mind coming along and help search for a town or something ?"

"No, not at all John," she replied letting his hand go, "I could use some real food anyway, you know…burgers and a beer…" John laughed, and gave her a big smile.

"Yeah, I could use a cool one, myself," he said, laughing. "I really appreciate you volunteering Monica. Now if we could just get one or two more to join us."

"I could go, John." Hellen stated.

"Who would take care of Bernie?" he asked.

"Yeah, I guess you're right."

"I could go John!" Jimmy broke in, "I'm not scared."

"I'll bet you're not, Jimmy. But you've gotta take care of your mom and the rest of the camp, right?"

"Yeah you're right. Mom needs me, that's for sure." Sally gave Jimmy a big huge for that one.

"How about that Dave Cummings guy?" Monica suggested, "He seems like he could handle the job."

"I haven't seen him around since he was talking to that Pete guy last night, when they were headed out to search for help. I don't think he went them, do you?" He asked while looking around at everybody.

"No I don't think he did," Sally suggested.

"Okay, I'll walk around and look for a couple more

volunteers," John said.

"Oh, I'll go with," Hellen injected, as she jumped up from her seat and placed her arm through John's, not giving Monica a chance to butt in. Once they got out of earshot of the others, Hellen said to John,

"Ya know John, I was hoping somebody would have been back by now, with some help. I know it's only been a few hours but I was still hoping."

"Me too, Hellen. I was thinking that myself."

"Don't you think it would be better if you stayed here and waited?"

"I would like to, but I got this weird felling in the back of my head...I'll tell you what I'll do Hellen. I'll follow that path for two hours, and if I don't come across anybody, I will turn around and come back here. So the most that I'll be gone for...is four or five hours...sound good to you?"

"That sounds great John, I'll even make you some homemade soup."

"And what do you plan on using for ingredients ?" He laughed.

"You'll see, there's plenty of natural ingredients all around us." Hellen remarked, laughing out loud. They walked hand in hand now, talking to people in different groups and drifted farther away from the lean-to.

"Wow," John stated, looking at his watch: 11:15 a.m. "It's getting late Hellen, we better head back."

"Oh, your right, time flies when your having fun." She was getting giddy, she felt like a young woman again. She told herself, *don't be silly, you're just feeling this way because of the situation...He doesn't have feelings for you...Does he?*

They made their way back to the gang. The first thing Bernie noticed was the hand holding and the look on Hellen's face. She knew that Hellen "got bit by the love bug." A huge grin spread across her wrinkled old face,

"We better get moving John. It's getting late." Monica advised, "Oh, and by the way, I recruited another helper to assist us. Tom Franklin, meet John Collins." She announced, proudly.

As John was shaking hands with Tom he wondered if Tom could even walk a mile without collapsing. He was around five foot five, maybe a hundred and thirty pounds, soaking wet. His hand grip was like shaking hands with a wet wash rag. He reminded Jack of that character on the Andy Griffin show...Barney. *Yeah that's right, Barney Fife...*

"Nice to meet you Barney...oh...I mean Tom." John was a little embarrassed at that statement.

"Nice to meet you...John." Tom said nervously, as he was shaking his hand, "I like to help when I can, ya know, do my civic duty and all,"

John smiled and thought: *This should be interesting. Really interesting.*

"Everyone ready?" John asked.

"Yep," Tom replied, "Let's get on with our journey"

"Time to rock and roll!" Monica chimed in. They all said their good byes and turned as they walked away.

John started thinking as they walked along the narrow dirt road. He was amused at what Tom had said, *"let's get on with our journey...The journey of a life time."* Isn't that what the slogan said on the top of the train ticket? He wasn't sure, but he wondered about that...trip of a lifetime?...journey of lifetime?...something like that. And then his mind drifted to that guy, David Cummings. *I don't remember him at all, being on the train...in the crash...Not at all...and then he just shows up, at the first sign of trouble, with a snide look on his face.* He had a bad feeling about that guy...he couldn't put his finger on it...*Why, why was he here? Why?*

CHAPTER 3

DEAL WITH THE DEVIL

Pete Perry's team marched on. Joe Rodger's walked wearily along the side of the tracks, holding the flashlight in his right hand, trying to shine it for the guys so they wouldn't trip. He kept shaking and dropping the light, so they continued busting his balls. He wiped his sweaty forehead constantly, with a white handkerchief that his mother had given to him just before the trip. The other guys were ahead of him, talking loudly as they marched along. Every so often, they would break out in laughter. Joe knew they were talking about him. They were probably cracking jokes and having a grand old time. Joe's mind started wandering. He was definitely not in shape for this hike…He seemed to be falling farther and farther behind.

"Slow down a little, will you guys?" Joe panted, "I'm dying back here."

"Jesus, Joe, we're not going that fast." One of them yelled back and chuckled. Then the others joined him in harmony. Joe was getting pissed off. He put up with this bullshit all of his life. Always the last guy in line — the last one to be chosen to participate in baseball or football games when he was in grade school. He gave up on the idea when he entered high school. By that time all of his classmates nicknamed him, 'Porky.' His so called buddies made him sit with the girls on the school bus and shouted fat jokes at him. He resented those daily bus rides. They were agonizing to him. *Now they call it bullying.* He was the last one for everything.

To add to his misery, the Phys. Ed coach would make him take showers after gym class. That was the worst. The laughing got hysterical, pointing at the huge rolls of blubber on his belly, shouting out, "lard ass, fat ass, needle dick," all why they threw soap it him, snapped towels that stung like a son of bitch when they landed on his soft skin. Yeah, they sure were his "fun" years, *good fuckin' memories!* from high school. Remembering this, Joe worked himself up into a rage.

And the guys marched on...

His mother never used the word, "fat" around her Joey—he was perfect in her eyes. She would always say "a little chunky...stocky...big boned...A slight weight problem." That's how she would defend him against family and friends, especially on holidays and his birthday partys.

His uncle and cousins would shout out a quick wisecrack, or a fat-joke at Joey, and his mom would jump to his defense, "he's just stout...just has a little weight problem" and that always made it worse. Remembering this, Joe was winding even tighter.

And the guys marched on...

All the teasing...laughing...name calling...pushing...shoving...slaps on the gut...cracks on the back of the head, and then they would run down the hallway yelling "catch me if you can, FAT Boy!" Joe was damaged inside forever, from all the abuse, the short and fat jokes. *From everything.* He held it all in, didn't showed it on the outside. "Don't let it upset you, Joey..." mom would always tell him. But it always did. and it still does.

And the boys marched on…

But tonight it was really pissing him off. After all, this was his idea — his plan to form a search party, find some help, and then return to the crash site and save everybody! He would be the hero! *And now these pricks want to take that away from me…no fuckin' way.*

"I'm sick of this shit," Joe whispered to himself, "who do these assholes think they are?" he said a little louder. "This was my idea to follow the tracks."

Louder…

"My idea to get away from the losers back there at the campsite. And now these pricks are going to laugh at me! Make fun of ME!" Joe was raging. Sweat was rolling into his eyes, burning them, stinging them.

AND THE BOYS WERE MARCHING ON!!

Joe's head was swelling up…it was going to explode! He rubbed his temples profusely and then his burning eyes…he was in a full RAGE! Just then his foot got caught on a railroad tie. He stumbled and came down on one knee—CRACK! His knee hit something hard—white pain shot through his whole body.

AND THE BOYS KEPT MARCHING ON!!

"AHHHHH," he yelled out, when his knee hit the steel rail. His face smashed into the dirt of the railroad bed. His flashlight flew out of his hand, tumbled, then curved to the left and rolled to a sudden stop. Its beam of light shined through the musty air, hitting Joe square in his fat face. Then the light flickered and fizzled out, putting Joe into total darkness.

"JOE! What happened!? Where the fuck are you?" Pete hollered back towards the scream, bringing laughs from the guys.

Joe could taste the rancid sand and dirt combination, entering his mouth as his face slapped the ground. He tried to answer Pete and he started gagging and choking. The grit was jammed between his teeth and tongue, all the way to his throat. Just then, two guys pulled him up to the sitting position and started hitting him on his back. The dirt gushed out of his mouth, he coughed and upchucked a few times as they kept slapping his back...

"You okay Joe?" Harry asked, half-heartedly. Joe was still spitting and trying to catch his breath.

"Here, drink some water," Pete said, "I'll help you get that shit out of your mouth."

The other guy moved the torch a little closer to see if all the dirt was out of Joe's mouth. Joe took a big breath—he was scared shitless. They stopped slapping his back.

"You all right?" Pete asked again, "how ya feeling?"

Joe wasn't sure, he was still huffing and puffing. His knee was red hot and throbbing like a son of a bitch.

"Wow, this is bad!" Harry, shouted, "his knee is cut pretty deep!" Joe looked down. His pants were torn wide open revealing a bloody mess! The pain was excruciating. He went into full panic mode!

"AHHH...this is BAD isn't it Pete?" Joe cried out. Pete was pissed that Harry pointed out the severity of Joe's wound, and that he just had to lower the torch down so Joe could get a better look at it.

"It's not that bad, Joe," Pete said, trying to calm him down. "I think it looks a lot worse then it really is."

"What? Are you kidding," Harry blurted out, "are you seeing what I'm seeing?" Before Pete could answer, Joe cried out again,

"MAN, I think I'm losing a lot blood! I can feel it oozing down my leg!" Steve Sullivan interrupted to offer his two cents:

"Take it easy Joe, I will clean it up and stop the bleeding for you. I know first aid, so stay cool, man." Steve said confidently, which helped Joe started to calm down a little.

"I need the flashlight," Steve announced, "Where is it?"

"I dropped it when I tripped. I think it ended up over there." Joe said, pointing to a spot by a fallen tree. "Pete, would you look over there for the flashlight ?" Steve asked.

"Fuck it" Pete shouted, "He dropped it, let him find it…"

"How 'bout you Harry," Steve asked, "would you mind?" Harry looked at Pete for permission. Pete gave him a dirty look.

"I'm not gonna look for fat boy's flashlight. He dropped it, let him find it."

The two of them started laughing. "This isn't funny guys." Steve broke in, "I gotta clean his wound and get it wrapped up, so get me the goddamn flashlight."

"Come on Steve, lighten up, we're just busting fat boy's balls." Pete shot back.

"Well enough busting balls for now," Steve stated, "let's start a fire so I can see how bad his wound is. Somebody find that flashlight!" He demanded.

"Bullshit!" Pete shouted, "We gotta keep moving!"

He wasn't laughing anymore. He had a mean look on his face and the shadow's from the torch made him look meaner. "NOW, get up FAT BOY, and get moving, or we'll leave you behind to rot in hell." Pete looked like his blood pressure was blowing out of his ears, and then he added, "and I'm not fucking around, either." Harry was getting a little nervous.

Joe had finally snapped. "I CAN'T MOVE, you stupid bastard! And don't call me FAT BOY! I'm sick of takin' shit from everybody, and especially from you, Pete!" All those years of being teased, tormented, bullied, pushed around, and beat up had finally taken their toll. Joe didn't realize how bad it sounded. Even Pete was thrown back by Joe's rant. But he had to save face.

"Well, FAT BOY, we're moving the fuck on. With you, or without you. So you can stay right here asshole and sit there and DIE! Cause I don't give a flying fuck!"

Steve stood up, he couldn't believe his ears. He looked at Harry, who was also shocked.

"We can't just leave him here! He's bleeding bad!"

"Shut the fuck up Steve. If you don't want to leave him, then you can carry his lard ass on your back, or stay here and hold his fuckin' hand." Pete was ready to knock somebody on their ass. "Harry, you ready to go?"

"I guess so, Pete."

"Good then. Let's go, guys."

Steve was confused. He wasn't sure what to do. He looked at Joe and then the others. He shook his head and looked down at Joe.

"I'm sorry Joe, but I gotta go." He started to walk away. But then came back. Joe's face calmed down a little.

"As soon as we get to a town, or somewhere, I'll come back with help. I promise."

Joe was in tears. "STEVE! Don't leave me here! Steve!" he begged, "I'll die! PLEASE, please Steve...don't!"

"It's not that bad Joe, just keep pressure on it. You'll be okay." Steve said. "I'll be back Joe. Honest. I'll be back."

Steve turned away for the final time. He started jogging to catch up with the others. All Joe could see now were the shadows of the diminishing torches.

Blood continued to ooze out of his leg. The cool, damp, night air was setting in now. Joe began to shake. A stirring, subtle breeze hit him every few seconds. The chill felt like an ice cold hand, faintly, slipping around his body. He was now feeling sorry for himself. His anger subsided enough for him to think clearly now. He promised himself that those bastards would pay for leaving him here.

Joe Rodgers sat in the freezing, dark night, shaking from the cold dampness, and the morbid fear of bleeding to death, all alone. Warm tears rolled down his chubby cheeks, the same chubby cheeks that his aunt Millie used to pinch at all the family gatherings, and upon which she would give him a big kiss, and then wipe her lipstick off with her thumb.

He continued searching for the flashlight. He couldn't stand the darkness. His knee was throbbing and his bandage was soggy, he knew it was still bleeding but he was afraid to take off the makeshift bandage and peek under it to see how bad it was.

"Oh my GOD…I'm going to bleed to death!" He cried out into the empty darkness. "Those bastards left me here to die!"

He was sobbing uncontrollably now. He let it all out…all those years of name calling…all the fat jokes. All the humiliation was erupting out of him now, like vomit that was trapped in his guts for the last twenty five years. He puked all over himself. He continued to cry as he cleaned himself off, which was very difficult in the darkness.

"They left me here!" he squealed, "those dirty, fuckin'…bastards! …left me here to die."

SNAP!

Joe froze. He held his breath, hot tears still running down his soiled face. He slowly opened his tear filled eyes, and scanned the darkness, while holding his breath and listening intently for any sound or slight movement.

He sensed something was close by. He could *feel* it. He knew what he heard. A crisp breaking of a branch under the pressure of someone (*or something's*) foot…But who's foot…a bear…a dear…human…? Or was it the assholes coming back to scare him? Laugh at him? Joe was shaking uncontrollably now. Instinctively he closed his eyes…then, …very faintly…

"Joey…Joey…"

"Who's out there?" he quietly choked out, "Is somebody out there?"

"Joey…"

Was it just the wind scurrying through the drying leaves on the trees?

"Joey…"

"I know someone's there…so come out please," Joe pleaded. Nothing happened.

"It must be the wind." He whispered, trying to convince himself…just the wind.

SNAP!

His heart stopped. A flash of light hit him directly in his eyes. He thought he would shit himself.

"Ahhhhhhh!" he screamed, as he heard a low hissing laugh.

"Relax Joey, it's just me, Dave Cummings. You know, from the crash."

Joey slowly opened eyes. Dave was standing right in front of him, and now had his flashlight shining under his chin, looking like a ghoul.

"Did I scare you, Joey Boy?" Dave questioned with a grin.

"Jesus, Dave," Joe said with a nervous laugh, "you almost gave me a heart attack, you crazy son of a bitch."

Joe was shocked and pissed at the same time, but glad to see another human being and not some, big-assed bear looking for his next meal…

"What the hell are you doing out here all by yourself any-ways, Joey?"

"You won't believe it, I tripped and busted my knee and it's bleeding real bad, plus I lost my flashlight, I think its broke, and those bastards left me here to die!" He was breaking down into tears again.

"Calm down buddy, pull yourself together, Let me have a look at that knee." Dave said with confidence, making Joe feel much better. "Here, you hold the light on your knee." Dave suggested, handing it to Joe, "that's right, keep it right on the wound." He removed the soiled rag from the wound, revealing a three inch gash on Joe's knee. He study it intensively as though he were a doctor.

"How's it look Dave?"

"Not too bad," he answered, "and I have a first-aid kit from the train with me, so I think I can help you."

That calmed down Joe immensely, and he started thinking that Dave wasn't as bad as everybody said he was. Joe kept the light on Dave's fingers as he stitched up the wound. The pain seemed to disappear instantly.

"Almost done, Joey. How's it feel?"

"Great Dave. You're the answer to my prayers."

Dave got a kick out of that statement. *If this kid only knew.*

"Okay Joey, you're good as new. By the way, do you prefer Joe or Joey?"

"I prefer Joe, but coming from you, the guy who just saved my life...You can call me Joey anytime you want," he announced proudly. "You're the best, Dave."

"Well thank you Joey, I try to please."

"If you didn't happen to come out here, Dave, I would have definitely died."

"Don't mention it again pal. It was the least I could do. But I just can't believe those guys abandon you here to die, I just can't comprehended it," Dave said, shaking his head. "And I don't blame you for wanting to get even with those bastards."

"Oh, I'll get even some how." Joe said, "I'm gonna smash their heads in."

"I believe you Joey, ...and I can help arrange that for you." Dave said, working on Joey's emotions.

"What do you mean by that Dave?"

"Ah, come on now Joey, think about it for a minute, they

harassed you…belittled you…abandoned you here to bleed to death, wouldn't even start a fire to keep warm, no water and not even a fucking light so you could see. What kind of a decent person would do that?" Dave was building up to a full blown rant.

You're right Dave, YOU'RE RIGHT!" Joe was psyched up now. "I'LL GET EVEN WITH THOSE COCKSUCKERS!" Joe felt the adrenaline blasting though his veins.

"That a boy, Joey! Can you feel it? Feel the POWER!

"YES…IT FEELS GREAT!" Joe's blood was overtaken by his adrenaline—it was coursing through his body like a bolt of lighting! He leapt to his feet—not a pain in his body! He looked down at his leg—it was practically healed! His stomach was tightening up, and he swore that he was getting taller. He felt invincible! He felt like he could rip a tree out of the ground and break it in half over his knee. He was blown out of his fucking MIND!

Meanwhile, Dave was dancing around Joey! Chanting in a foreign tongue, creating a demonic force field around the both of them. Joey thought that Dave looked like a Witch Doctor on cocaine. Joe's heart was a burning inferno, fired from the blazes of Hell.

"HOW YOU FEELING, JOEY?" Dave screeched at the top of his lungs. "Are you with me BOY! DO YOU WANT REVENGE, JOEY?"

"YES! I'm with you! Anything you say, Dave! Anything you WANT! I AM WITH YOU!" Joey was completely out of his mind, feeding on the new power, that was racing through his burning arteries—he was amped up to the MAX! Ready to do the nasty DEED. The king of hell was in full control now, and David was ready to do his bidding.

"Whatever you need Dave, whatever it takes!" Joe said, looking at Dave intensely.

"Just a mere hand shake Joe," he declared, with an evil smile, "in exchange for your soul, you can live out all of your dreams and get all the revenge that you want." David held out his hand.

Joe shook it, without the least bit of hesitation. David screamed at the top of his lungs.

"DONE DEAL! DONE DEAL MOTHER FUCKER!" They held the hand shake for what seemed like an hour to Joe. Joe felt a burst of power surging through his arm and over his entire body—ten fold of what he felt before!

He felt indestructible—he was going through some kind of demonic metamorphosis! Finally, David released Joe's hand, then threw something to the ground. When it hit, it sparked and instantly burst into a bonfire. Joey was loving every second of it…

Come on baby, light my fire…
Tried to set the night on fire…
So come on baby light my fire…

"Come on Joey, dance with me…"

Joey jumped up—six feet off the ground—and began to dance wildly in a circle with David. He was over the edge of reality now, as they spun faster and faster, creating a small twister of smoke and fire. Demons joined in with them, dancing and laughing in their satanic ritual.

"What kind of dance is this, Dave?" Joey screamed, while inhaling the raw smoke.

It's the dance of the beast!

They barked at the moon, as they spun in circles. Flames from the fire shot up high and licked their skin, burning their flesh. Screeching, raving, chanting, preparing for the HUNT. Preparing for the KILL.

The kill of a life time.

"Ready for your revenge, Joey?" he asked with an evil smirk across his hellish face.

"Let's go pal," Joe answered him, "Lead me to the Lambs, and I'll do the slaughtering."

Joe was all wound up and ready for the kill. Joe eagerly followed behind David, like a pet dog. Walking at first, then they started to jog. At Joey's request, they began to run, faster and faster until the trees and bushes were nothing but a blur. Joey was on a power high, he felt extremely strong, leaping like a panther, pursuing its next prey. He leaped twenty feet or more, then sprung off the ground again, landing on a boulder and screeched like a mad banshee.

"THERE THEY ARE JOEY!" David howled, "ripe for the picking, just like I promised you!"

"GREAT, I'll get my revenge now! They will pay the price NOW!" Joey hollered as he flew into Pete's back, smashing him into the ground. Then he reached around Pete's head and with one quick twist he snapped his neck like a toothpick. Then he stood up slowly, turned and walked over to Harry and Steve and placed his hands on his hips.

"Remember me, assholes?" They thought that they were going mad. "IT'S ME, Joey the fat ass!" They couldn't believe their eyes…It was Joe, alright, but with muscles, and he was taller. He took a step closer to them and leaned forward until his nose almost touched Harry's nose

"Joey?" Harry whispered.

"That's JOE to you!" Joe shouted, "only Dave Cummings can call me Joey!"

Joe threw a vicious uppercut into Harry's jaw, knocking him off his feet. As he fell to the ground, three of his teeth flew out of his now bloodied mouth. Then he grabbed him off the ground and torpedoed him head first into an oak tree! Harry's skull cracked open on impact, with blood pouring out of his head and slowly down the trunk of the oak tree. Joey then turned towards Steve.

"Take it easy, Joe," Steve pleaded, "I was the one who helped you, remember. It was all Pete's idea to leave you behind... And I didn't want to go, but...ah...I had to, you know how it is...don't you...Joe...

"SHUT UP STEVE! You laughed at me too, and called me names right along with them, so your going to pay the price too!"

"Hold on Joey," David interjected, and stepped between Joe and Steve. "Calm down a little bit."

"I'll calm down when this asshole is dead."

"Please Joe," Steve begged, "I helped you...I was coming back for you...honest Joe..." Steve fell to his knees and started crying. Then he looked at David, "Please David, can't you talk some sense into him?"

"Tell you what, Steve, if you join the club, I'll talk Joey into sparing your life."

"What the hell are you talking about?" Joey protested, "you promised that I could get my revenge!"

"I know Joey and you will, just hear me out..." David assured. Joey gave him a affirmative nod. Steve was dumbfounded, and didn't have glue of what was going on.

"Now listen up, the both of you." David said in an eerie voice. "Steve, you screwed Joey over last night and left him to die." Steve stood still and he was shaking his head. "I just happened to stumble on Joey and was able to help." David was now grinning. "You may have noticed some changes in him, for the better, I might add." Again, that evil smirk. "Now I can try to hold him back, but...I *did* make a deal with him. And, one thing is—I *never* break a deal. So I guess if you want to stay in one piece, you'll have to make a deal too."

Steve looked up at David and then at Joey.

"What do I have to do?" he asked meekly.

"It's simple Steve," David stated, with a satanic smile spreading over his face. "All I require is a simple handshake, ...*a deal, if you wish,* and you will have all the things you've ever wanted, for as long as you live...money, women, super strength. Just like Joey over there..." David said, looking over at Joey, "...he looks like a pro wrestler, doesn't he? Wouldn't you want to look like that?"

Steve's head was spinning. He figured he didn't have much of a choice.

"Okay, I'm in." Steve conceded, and shook hands with David. "I'll take your deal, just keep Joe away from...please..."

"Good, then it's a deal," David confirmed, accepting Steve's handshake. "Very good, very good indeed. Your soul for health and wealth and a lifetime of pleasure."

"Whaddaya mean, 'my soul?' " Steve asked.

"Who cares, Steve? He's gonna give us anything we want forever, and I won't even tear you apart!" laughed Joey. "So you have nothing to lose."

Steve was screwed either way, so he nodded his head in agreement and cracked a smile.

"DONE DEAL!" David screamed again. "LET'S PARTY BOYS!" And with a flick of his wrist, a bonfire appeared shooting flames and smoke high into the air. As they howled and danced around the blazing flames, Steve thought to himself how they reminded him of a scorching inferno.

Little did he know: HE would be the sacrificial lamb.

Around and around the fire they danced, getting stronger and more deranged by the second. Joey and Steve were going to like this new life.

The Truth

After their party, David and the boys settled down and started talking about their future. Money, booze, drugs, women, rock 'n roll, and...*oh yeah...*

"Before you get to involved with your future, guys," David said, "there's something you need to know."

"What's that pal?" Joey asked.

"Well, to start off with, I'm on a mission to collect souls. I only need seven more of them to complete my deal with 'the man.'"

"The man?" Joey asked, "but *you are* 'the man,' aren't ya?"

"Ha, not me, Joey," David started laughing. "I'm just a grain of sand, son, doin' my job, helpin' out as much as I can. Know what I mean?"

"What the hell is that supposed to mean?" Joey yelled. "I thought you were the boss? You were Mister Big Fuckin' Shot. Who are you shitting?"

"Hey, I didn't lie to you guys. I'm keeping all the promises I made. I'm going to fulfill everyone of them." David snickered.

"Fulfill? What, are you kidding me! You haven't fulfilled shit!" Joey hollered. "What about all those promises you made, women, money, fast cars, and all the rest of your bull shit. What about it?"

"Calm down Joey, You don't see Steve losing his cool, do ya? And I will definitely hold up my end of the deal. You will get all that stuff...for as long as you live.

David was building up to an frenzy now. "So what, you're gonna kill us now?" Joey demanded.

"NO, no, no, don't be silly Joey. *You're already dead.* You have been for almost forty hours now." Steve and Joey fell to their knees, confused. David grinned and looked at his watch, "Well boys, I hate to run, but I gotta get going. More souls to collect—*you know it is*." He was hysterical by now. He started to walk away.

"Wait, wait, what's going to happen to us?" Steve cried out.

"Ohhhhhh. I'd rather not think about that one, guys."

"And what do you mean, we're already dead?" Joey added.

"You'll see soon enough. I don't have the time to explain it now, but you'll see soon enough."

David walked away and disappeared into the woods.

CHAPTER 4

THE JOURNEY

Dan, Hank, Patti & Jerry, and Eli started off their journey on a good note. They were content on going for help and felt they were doing a good deed. Their torches burned slowly and provided ample light as they walked along the abandoned elevated railroad bed. After walking a short distance, they spotted some twisted rails that looked like they were deliberately ripped up and placed to the side. The tracks then continued to straighten out and looked good enough to actually run a train on them. They stopped for a minute to examine the situation. Eli squatted down and lowered the torch within a foot of the track. Hank and Dan looked over his shoulder and watched him carefully. Patti and Jerry stood back wondering what they were doing.

"I wonder why that one section of track was torn out?" Dan asked. "Especially if the train runs through here twice a day."

"Yeah, it doesn't make sense, does it?" Hank added.

"Let's think this over carefully." Eli commented. "First the tracks were torn up at the crash site, which is approximately and half a mile from here, give or take. Then you gotta ask yourself, were they deliberately torn up, or maybe they were just worn out. Also I noticed, there is no eight-foot wire fence, enclosing the tracks in. So I don't think they would run the Silver Streak on these tracks."

That made sense to Dan and Hank.

"So the only logical explanation I come up with," Eli continued, "is somehow the Silver Streak had to switch tracks at some point and end up on this old section of rails."

Eli moved up the tracks a little further, and intensely studied them. "Look here," he said, pointing towards the ground, "the railroad ties are old and rotted. Some of them are totally gone, nothing but saw dust. And some of the tracks themselves, are missing spikes. I don't think these tracks have been used in years."

"So how in the hell did we get stuck on them?" Hank asked anxiously.

"My best guess is," Eli stated, "somewhere back on the line, the train was mistakenly switched over to this line and the engineer didn't notice. He didn't reduce the speed because he didn't realize that he was on the wrong line."

"Maybe he fell asleep, like the rest of us, and the rest is history." Dan commented.

"That's a possibility," Eli stated, "but I doubt it." He checked his cell phone to see what time it was. "Ah shit, my cell is dead. Any of you guys got the time?"

Just then Patti cut in, "It's 9:36."

"Geez, it's getting late," Dan stated, "we better get a move on if going to find some help." They all agreed to that.

The night became very still, and there was an eerie chill engulfing them as they walked along the old railroad tracks. The torches had dwindled and then finally burned out, making it more difficult to walk. Trying not to trip over anything, they decided to walk on the railroad ties and keep close.

"Hey look guys," Hank said, pointing toward the sky. "The

moon is coming out from behind the clouds."

"We finally got a break." Jerry said.

"And it's about time we gotta little luck." Patti added.

"And speaking of a luck," Eli said, "is that a light or just a reflection of the moon?"

"Where?" Dan asked.

"Right over there, just to the left, about three hundred yards up ahead." Everyone got excited, and Patti got a little giddy.

"Let's check it out." Dan suggested.

They eagerly followed the tracks, moving closer to the light, which soon became lights, and then became silhouettes of buildings. Their prayers of finding help were answered!

They stepped over the rail and headed down a narrow path that lead into the small village. As they approached the first house they noticed an old man sitting on a rickety old rocking chair. He didn't move a muscle—apparently, he was sleeping. He had a corn cob pipe dangling out of his mouth, old and faded bib overalls, a flannel shirt with the sleeve rolled up, and a pair of deer-skin slippers. Hanging down from the porch ceiling was an old light bulb with a couple of bugs flying around it. The paint on the old wood siding was cracked and curled. The rotting porch steps leaned to the left and were in desperate need of repair. This whole scene was illuminated by that old, dingy light bulb—it could have been a Norman Rockwell painting.

"This house must be a hundred years old." Hank said.

"Yeah," Dan responded, "looks like a old mining town."

"Who wants to wake up the old guy?" Eli asked.

"I'll do the honors," Dan replied.

Dan carefully climbed up the rotting steps. "Hello, sir… excuse me sir, hello…" He leaned in slowly towards the old man. He didn't want to give the old geezer a heart attack. "Hello…Hello sir…"

Dan turned around and said, "I think the old buck is dead," he said, "should I shake him?"

"No, let's try another house, we don't want to rile him up." Eli stated. Dan carefully stepped off the porch and they all walked down the dirt road for a bit before they came to the next house. The scene was the same: paint peeling off the siding, dirty windows, pickets dangling from the handrails, and so on.

"Wow, this town needs a face lift." Hank said, "Who wants to knock on the door?"

"I did the last one." Dan quickly replied.

"I'll do it," Jerry volunteered, as he sprung onto the porch deck. He knocked a few times, and waited for a response. Soon enough, the door slowly creeked open. An elderly woman appeared.

"Who's there?"

Jerry was a taken aback. "Hi ma'am. Could…"

"Who's there?" she interrupted.

"Ma'am, I'm right here." Jerry replied.

"Who's there!?" the old woman persisted. "Is that you— is that the Collin boys? If it is, I'm gonna tell your parents, and they'll take a switch to your backsides!" She was getting aggravated by now. She looked side-to-side, then slammed the door shut with a disgusting look on her face.

"What the hell was that all about?" Jerry asked.

"Beats me," Dan answered, "but peek through the window and see what's she up to."

"No way," Jerry replied, "this is to spooky for me." And he jumped off the porch, and started walking away. "Let's try another one," he said, "and this time somebody else can knock."

Hank moved up to the door at the next house, and started knocking, Nothing. Nobody came to the door and he was knocking hard.

"Let's try another one!" Hank said, getting pissed. They

moved to another street, stopped, and looked the situation over.

"Over there, there's a light on." Hank said, pointing towards a larger home, half way down the street. The house was as large as a hotel, and it was in very good shape. The exterior was nicely painted. There were fresh flowers in full bloom, sprouting out of the wooden flower boxes, that were attached to the banisters. There were three pendent lights attached to the porch ceiling, cascading down a soothing glow of warm, soft light, making the home very inviting. They all drew near the welcoming front porch.

This time Eli did the knocking. There was a large brass door knocker located in the center of a beautiful, stained oak door. Eli grasped it and firmly began to knock on the door. Out of nowhere two large black dogs began barking and ran towards them—immediately lights shined through the paned glass windows which overlooked the front porch. A large woman burst through the front door and started screaming into Eli's surprised face.

"WHO'S OUT THERE!? WHO'S OUT THERE!?"

Eli was in total disbelief—she was looking *right at him,* not a foot between them! And she was acting like she didn't see him!

"What the hell is your problem, lady?" Eli screamed. He turned to the others, "Is she fucking blind!" Just then, the dogs scaled the front porch—their eyes were as black as coal, their ears pointed straight up and saliva gushed from their gnashing white teeth. Eli kicked the first one, and Hank threw a rock at the second one.

"LET'S GET THE HELL OUT OF HERE!" Dan yelled.

"Good idea," Eli agreed. They all jumped off the porch and ran like hell in the direction of the dirt road where they came in at. The fat lady came outside again, this time armed with a shotgun.

BOOM!

By now more dogs were chasing them and coming from all directions. More lights flashed on. People started stepping out off their homes, half dressed and asleep.

Hank yelled "FASTER GUYS! The dogs are catching up!"

They started passing the first house and the old man was getting off his rocking chair and yelled "WHO'S OUT THERE!?"

"It's just us, old man!" Jerry yelled back. "We could use some help!"

The old man paid no attention to them, he just kept yelling. Then he turned and headed inside his house, yelling, "Martha! Get my shotgun!"

"Faster guys! I hear more dogs coming!" Dan yelled. They picked up their pace.

"What the hell is wrong with these assholes!?" Hank hollered as they reached the railroad tracks...

"I don't know," Eli replied, "but those dogs are almost on us," Patti said, trying to catch her breath

Jerry put his arm around her. "You okay sis?"

"I'm good," she panted. "Let's just go, I don't want to be bitten by those vicious dogs or shot by those crazy people!"

"I hear ya sis...let's go." They caught their breath and started running again.

Dan tripped, yelling as he hit the train rail. Hank and Eli quickly picked him up.

"Come on, keep moving."

Dan tried his best but his ankle was throbbing. The dogs caught up to them, and started nipping their legs and ankles. Hank kicked one of them in the stomach and it ran away into the night howling. The other dogs backed off a little bit. Patti and Jerry picked up some rocks and threw them, landing some good shots. That pretty much broke up the dog chase. Everyone was out of breath and they slowed down to a fast walk.

"I'm getting too old for this shit," Hank confessed between breaths

"I gotta slow down too," Dan agreed. "My ankle is swollen up and is killing me." They sat down and took a well-deserved break. When they started to catch their breath, Eli pointed back towards the town.

"Now what the hell is that?" He exclaimed. "Look at all those moving lights. What are they?"

"Beats the hell outta me," Hank replied.

"I don't believe it" Dan said, "they're following us."

"WHO?" Hank asked.

"The townspeople." Dan said.

"No way," Hank shot back, "they wouldn't even talk to us, so why the hell would they follow us?"

"I'm not sure, but they're coming. We'd better get out of here fast." Eli suggested. Before the words got out of his mouth, the dogs started howling again. They all started running again, with the exception of Dan, who limped as quickly as he could.

"What is their problem?" Hank questioned, "You'd swear that we killed somebody or something."

"Pick it up guys," Eli urged them, "I'm sure we can outrun those old buzzards."

The moon was full and high in the sky by now, casting long black shadows of the trees over the railroad tracks and the search party. They stopped for a breather and to observe the progress of the townspeople. They could still see the twinkling of their flashlights, and, every now and then, hear the howling of the dogs.

"We should be back at the campsite pretty soon, right Dan?" Hank asked.

"I'd say in another thirty minutes or so. You know, I would

have thought those old bastards would have giving up by now."

As they walked further down the tracks, they spotted the welcoming glow of warm campfires. Dan smiled and thought that it would be good to get back and tell everyone about their crazy adventure. Then he looked back in the other direction.

"I can't believe it," Dan exclaimed, "those crazy bastards are still coming."

Eli turned around and took a look for himself, "They sure are a determined bunch of old hoots, aren't they?" he said.

"Let's pick up the pace and head for camp," Dan said.

"Hold on a sec," Eli interrupted, "do we really want those crazy bastards following us all the way to the camp?"

"That might a good point. You're probably right," Dan said.

"So what do you think we should do?" Hank asked, while scratching his head.

"I suppose we'll have to make a stand." Eli proposed.

"What's that mean?" Patti nervously asked.

"It means that we will just wait here and try to see what their problem is," Eli answered.

"And then what?" Hank anxiously asked.

"And then we will try to calm them down. Once we do that, I'm sure they'll help us, especially when we show them the crash site and the wounded," Eli responded.

The barking of the dogs turned into growls, and when the townspeople got closer to them, the dogs went crazy and started snapping and biting. The old timers couldn't see what was causing the dogs to go into a frenzy but they started yelling and shaking their fists in the air. Suddenly, gunshots started ringing out. Eli couldn't believe it…

"Why the hell are they shooting at us!?" He shouted.

"Beats me," Hank answered," But let's get hell out of Dodge!"

Before they could move, Dan got bit hard on his ankle.

Another dog jumped up and knocked over Jerry as it gnawed on his arm. Things were looking bad. The old timers were shooting at them, fortunately missing their shots. They were only standing twenty feet away from the old fools, but the gunshots continued to miss them. Hank and Patti managed to get the dogs off of Jerry and Dan. Eli grabbed an old tree limb that was laying near the tracks and slammed it into three of the dogs, scaring the rest of the pack back. The shooting stopped temporarily as old bastards reloaded their rifles. Eli reached down and gave Dan a hand up,

"Come on, let's get out of here—before they have time to reload!"

"Sounds good to me," Dan shouted, and they all ran as fast as they could down the tracks. It was daybreak when they entered the camp site…

"What's going on Dan?" Hellen asked, "we heard gunshots!"

"I'm not sure Hellen." Dan replied, "But we gotta get out of here! Sally, get Jimmy, and I'll get Bernie—we gotta go NOW."

Hank and Jerry started to round up the rest of the folks. Eli and Patti went to help the wounded collect their things and help them get on their feet and start moving.

"Let's go! Gotta move!" Dan ordered.

"Where to, Dan?" Sally inquired. "Which way?"

"Dan," Eli shouted, "I spotted some foothills over there. Let's go that way."

"Sounds go to me," Dan said, and they headed off in that direction. When they all made it to the foothills, Eli instructed them to hide behind some trees and large rocks for their protection.

"What to you think Eli? Are we safe?" Dan whispered.

"For now I guess…I'm not sure…"

The group was, for the most part, totally confused. They had no idea what was happening. Hellen kept her arm around

Bernie, who comforted her and told her everything was going to be all right.

"LOOK DAN!" Jimmy shouted, "It's the police! We're saved!"

Everyone turned and looked down, then someone in the group shouted that they rush down to them. Most of the group jumped up and started sprinting down the hill to what they thought would be safety. Dan shot his arm out in an effort to stop the rest of them.

"HOLD ON, not so fast!" He shouted, "something just isn't right!"

"What do you mean Dan?" Hank asked.

"I'm not sure, but something isn't right..."

"I have that feeling, too." Eli said. "This whole thing is screwed up. Let's just stay here for a while and see what happens."

The group reluctantly complied, but they trusted Dan's judgement.

AND THE SUN BEGAN TO SHINE

It was chaos—the townspeople were arguing with the police while the police tried to calm them down and take their guns, while the dogs just kept on yapping at all of them.

"Absolute Mayhem," Eli whispered, "I've never seen anything like that. You, Dan?"

"Nope. Damned if I can figure it out."

More flashing lights joined the scene as it got even crazier. One thing Dan noticed was that nobody was helping the crash victims. They were checking out the surrounding area, the smoldering camp fires, the broken tracks, but not the casualties. It didn't make sense.

"Dan," Hank said, pointing at the cops and the old folk,

"looks like their coming again, and this time their bringing the calvary with them."

"Maybe we should send up a white flag or something." Eli suggested.

Just then, an unmarked car pulled up. It was black and had no flashing lights. Three men and one women exited the car, and walked over to one of the officers.

"Hey guys," Eli mentioned, "we must be important, looks like the FBI is here."

"Are you kidding," Hank asked, "just what the hell did we do?"

"I don't know but it must of been good," Eli replied.

"Let's make our way up the mountain," Dan urged, "we'll be safer up there and have a better view of everything."

Without question, they all followed Dan up the mountain side. It was a nice, groomed trail, making it an easy climb. Jimmy was getting tired, so Dan lifted him up and sat him on his shoulders. As they continued to climb, Eli kept watch on the progress of the police and townsfolk below.

"They're still coming," Eli reported, "about two hundred yards back, but it looks like they may be slowing down."

"That's good," Hank replied, "because I sure could use a rest."

"Me too." Jimmy chimed in.

"What do you mean, 'me too?'" Dan said. "I'm the one doing all the work." Everybody laughed.

"They're stopping." Eli announced. "Looks like they are arguing with the townsfolk again. I guess we can take a break."

Everybody sat down and took a well-deserved break. Sally and Hank passed out some water and what little food they had left. After Dan removed Jimmy from his aching shoulders, he sat down and leaned back against a tree and stretched out his legs. He started to think about the events of last couple days.

Traveling on a great train to go visit my daughter in California. Then the train crashs. Then the disappearing passengers, the crazy bitch barfing on me in the back of the train. Camp. Then those crazy old bastards from the town, first ignoring us, then chasing us. Now, the FBI and every other nitwit comes along. What the hell else could happen next?

CHAPTER 5

AND THE HEADLINES
READ

TRAIN CRASH KILLS 67 PASSENGERS
AND 8 CREW MEMBERS

THE SILVER STREAK TRAIN derailed and plunged 190 feet into a rocky ravine just east of Pittsburgh, Pa. An explosion collapsed a fifty year old train trestle, at approx. 10:20 this morning. FBI, State and Local Police, are investigating the crash scene. This could be the worst train mishap in twenty years. Due to the rain and fog, search and rescue operations are hindered. Several victims still not accounted for. Homeland Security has been called in, due to the possibility of a terrorist threats against the United States.

Crash site: Kurtzville, Pa.

THREE HOURS AFTER THE CRASH

"Agent Pierce and Harris," Captain Lewis stated, from the Kurtzville police department, "this is Patrolman Mark Hunter. He was the first officer on the scene this morning." Captain Lewis didn't like strangers stepping on his jurisdiction in his quiet little town of Kurtzville, but the mayor had called him about a hour ago and laid down the law.

"Thank you, Captain." Agent Ann Pierce replied, while shaking hands with Mark Hunter. "As you know, this is my partner, Ted Harris."

"So, what do we have here?" Harris asked, shaking hands with Hunter.

"Well," he swallowed, "I gotta tell ya, I'm a little intimidated by you FBI agents. I'm not used to working with you big guns."

"Hey Mark," Harris said, with a grin, "we all put our pants on one leg at a time. So tell me, what's up?"

"It's the damndest thing," Mark replied, "I think some of the passengers are missing."

"You mean that you haven't found them yet, right?" Agent Harris said. "You're searching through the wreck, but you haven't found them. Do you think they might have wondered off?"

"No, I don't think anyone survived the crash, let alone wandered off." Hunter shot back.

"Slow down cowboy," Harris countered, "how 'bout starting from the beginning. You know, like, when you arrive, the conditions, et cetera. Okay?

"Okay," Hunter agreed, "Let's see, …I received the 911 at approximately 10:30 a.m. I arrived at the scene…ah… about 10:43. The flames and the smoke were unbelievable! I approached the edge of the ravine and couldn't believe my eyes. There were two mangled train cars at the bottom, engulfed in flames! I radioed for fire rescue and the state police. Then

I went back to my cruiser and grabbed my rain gear and face mask out of the trunk. I returned to the edge and made my way down to the crash site." Hunter took a deep breath, and looked around at the news media and probably a hundred bystanders. They were pushing against the police line trying to get a better view of the crash. He was getting tired—he had made at least ten trips up and down the ravine so far, hauling equipment and supplies for the state police and volunteer firemen. His twenty-seven year old body felt like it was sixty…

"Officer Hunter…?" Agent Pierce asked, snapping her fingers in front of his face, interrupting his thoughts."Hello?"

Hunter snapped out of it.

"Oh, yeah…sorry…ah, where was I?"

Agent Pierce got frustrated and said, "You were making your way down the embankment…and…" Agent Harris shook his head and rolled his eyes in disbelief.

"Oh, ahh,yeah, I went down the embankment to look for survivors…but everybody that I saw was dead. Then it started raining, to make things worse."

"If everybody was dead, according to you, where did the report of sixty missing passenger's and eight missing crew member's originate from?" Harris asked.

"Ah, that was sixty-seven missing passengers, I think, sir." Hunter shot back, "I believe someone from the railroad faxed over a passenger list to us, and I did a headcount."

"And that's what you came up with?" Harris asked.

"On the list that they faxed, there were one hundred thirty passengers and twelve crew members. We've only found seventy five bodies so far and they were burnt pretty bad. The only way we recognized the crew members was by their metal name badges, so we don't know where the others are." Hunter explained.

"Maybe they just got off at the last station stop." Pierce stated.

"I checked that already," Hunter said, "a couple of people boarded the train, but nobody got off at the last stop." Pierce had a puzzled look on her face, then Hunter suggested that they all go down and check out the scene.

"You and officer Hunter go down," Harris said, "I'll be with you in a few minutes. I'm going over to check out the train trussell and see what kind of explosives was used. It might give me an idea what we are up against." Harris walked away and pulled out his notepad, and was mumbling to himself.

Pierce and Hunter moved slowly down the steep bank towards the wreck. There were emergency lights set up everywhere, with bright yellow extension cords going from one to the other, and then to a portable generator. Two-way radios and phones were crackling and beeping with questions and orders from above.

There was a team of ten fireman hauling body bags from the wreck onto stretchers, then up the embankment. As the rain hit the flames of the wreck, it hissed and created smoke and steam that lingered all around, keeping visibility at a bare minimum. The hope was draining out of the eyes of the search and rescue workers as they looked at more of the bodies.

Hunter was scanning the area slowly. Pierce turned quickly, thinking she heard something: a small cry? Maybe just a stray cat? Hunter gave her a quick look thinking that she lost her balance or something.

"You okay?" He asked her.

"Shh! I think I heard a cry," she whispered. She slowly started walking in the direction of the noise. Hunter followed her. She came to a pile of twisted steel, glass, ripped seats and other debris. Hunter came to her side. She knelt down very slowly. She tipped her head and listened closely. She heard it again…faintly…faintly …but she was sure that she heard it… Her instincts told her that someone was close by.

"Give me a hand moving this stuff," she asked Hunter, handing him a piece of a burnt seat. Piece by piece, they carefully moved the twisted metal. They got to a door or a roof section of shredded metal and couldn't move it. Hunter got on his two-way and called for assistance. It took five of them to clear it out of the way. When the heap was cleared, they discovered a woman and a little girl laying next to each other, on the ground. The little girl was crying, and the woman didn't show any signs of life. The little girl was covered in a thin layer of dust and soot. Pierce reached down and gently picked her up, and pushed back her tangled hair. The girl gave a sigh of relief and wrapped her arms around Pierce's neck.

"You're going to be all right, sweety." Pierce said. "Is that your mommy?"

She nodded her head and whispered yes, then started to cry.

Pierce looked at Hunter, and motioned him to check out the woman. He quickly got down and placed his two fingers on her neck. To his surprise, he felt a faint pulse!

"She has a pulse!" He grabbed his two-way radio, "Get a medic over here, STAT!" Officers started yelling and waving directions to their location. Hunter keyed up his radio again, "We have two survivors over here!"

"Say again?" Came a reply from top side.

"We found two survivors! A little girl, approximately 9 or 10 years old, and her mother, early thirty's. The girl appears to be in fair condition and the mother, unconscious…slight pulse…the medic's just arrived and are attending her now."

Just then a news chopper appeared overhead, flying low with two spotlights scanning the site. The camera man was hanging out of the sliding door, holding on with one hand and filming with his other hand. They were so low that the chopper blades were kicking up small debris and swirled the thick smoke, creating a wind funnel.

"That's just what we need," agent Hunter yelled. "More noise and scattering the evidence all over the place—somebody get that chopper out of here!"

"There may be more survivors in this mess but we're never going to find them with all this noise!" Pierce added. Hunter got on the horn and gave the orders to "get that friggin' chopper out of here."

"Who the hell are you giving orders to?" Captain Lucas called back to Hunter. Pierce overheard Lucas's demand, and she snapped.

"Give me that two way." She demanded, grabbing the phone with one hand and holding onto the little girl with the other. "Captain Lucas! This is Agent Pierce! Get that chopper out of here and tell your men to get the reporters and civilians out of this ravine! If you can't do that, then tell whoever's in charge of this rescue mission to do it! Do you copy me?"

"10-4" is all the captain had to say.

"Mommy, mommy, where's my mommy?" The little girl cried out!

"She's right over there honey." Pierce said, pointing to the crew. "She's going to be all right. They are getting her ready to go up the hill and then to the hospital."

The girl's breathing slowed down and she started looking almost calm. Pierce introduced herself: "My name is Ann, what's yours?"

"Amy Beckman," she replied softly, "but mommy says I'm not supposed to talk to strangers."

"It's OK sweetie, I am a police officer. See?" Pierce said, showing Amy her identification badge,

"F. B. I. ?" Amy asked, "you mean like on TV?"

"Yes, that's right honey, just like on TV. So would you like to help me, sweetie?"

"Sure." Amy answered, "what do you want me to do?"

"Do you think you can help me and officer Hunter climb up that steep bank?" Before Amy could answer her, Pierce introduced her to Hunter, "Amy, this is Officer Hunter."

"Hi Amy," Hunter said and held out his hand to her, "you can call me Mark, okay? Now hold my hand and we'll see if we can make it up this steep hill, alright?"

"Ok, that sounds good to me, Officer Mark" she replied with a slight smile.

They finally made it to the top of the ravine just as they were placing Amy's mother into the ambulance. Amy ran towards the ambulance, and shouted back to Pierce,

"Can I ride in the ambulance with my mommy?"

Pierce noticed that there were two paramedics working on Amy's mother and that it didn't look good.

"How about we follow behind, honey? There are a lot of doctors in there helping mommy."

Amy managed a smile and reluctantly nodded her head. The three of them got into Mark's police cruiser and followed closely behind the ambulance, all on their way to the hospital.

"Amy, do you think you can tell me what happened on the train?" Mark asked, as they were driving down the highway.

"I guess so. I was playing with my doll, Sarah…oh, oh, Sarah, …where is she? We have to go back down and find Sarah!"

"Don't worry sweetie, we'll find Sarah for you, I promise." Hunter said as they continued to drive to the hospital. "So tell us what you remember."

"Alright," she answered, "I was playing with Sarah and having fun in my seat. Mommy was reading her book. Then I heard a big noise. It was real loud, like thunder, and then the train started to shake. I got scared and jumped on my mommy's lap and her soda spilled all over the floor! Then it felt like we were flying in an airplane! Mommy was real scared too. All the lights went out, and that's all I remember."

They arrived at the hospital and checked in, then they had the long wait for the ER people to examine Amy. Hunter took this time to make a few phone calls to the station and the crash site.

"Can I go in and see my mommy now, Amy?"

"Sure honey, just let me check with the doctor and I will ask him if mommy is ready for a visit, okay?" Amy nodded her head. Ann went to the nurses station to see about the condition of Amy's mother and asked to see the doctor on call.

Agent Ted Harris spent the better part of three hours working with the bomb squad and the state police, searching for traces of what type or types of explosives had been used to blow up the train trussell.

"Looks like a real professional job," one of the officers suggested and another officer agreed. Harris didn't agree, but he kept it to himself. They continued searching the area for more clues. Then Harris spotted something in the mud, just a fragment of metal was showing on the surface...

"Check this out guys," Harris said, bending down and very carefully picking up the piece of metal by its edge. He carefully lifted it up and out of the slimy mud. "Looks like a piece of detonator." They came over and one of the bomb squad guys opened up a plastic bag. Harris carefully dropped the jagged piece of metal into the bag.

"Keep looking guys. I'm sure you will find more of these fragments in the immediate area. I have to go find my partner and finish my report. If you come up with anything else, let me know. Here's my cell number."

Harris pulled up the collar on his coat, and cursed the drizzling rain. He walked back over to the main crash site, and slowly making his way down the steep and slippery ravine. He tried to wipe the mud off of his shoes, then started asking more questions and recording notes on his phone. His cell phone beeped, interrupting his train of thought.

"Harris, it's me. We're at the hospital. We found two survivors—a little girl and her mother."

"I was beginning to wonder where you were, Pierce. I heard something about survivors. Are they okay?"

"The little girl is fine. She's in with the ER doctor right now. Her mother is stabilized but not out of the woods yet. Are you still at the crash site? Did they find any more survivors or bodies?"

"Yes, I'm still at the site, and no, no more bodies yet. It beats the hell out of me, Pierce. They have to be here—they couldn't just get up and walk away. Did you get any information from the little girl?"

"Not much. Nothing that we couldn't have guessed at, anyway. So what's it all mean Harris? Did you come up with any theory's yet?…Harris…Harris …are you there?"

"Ah, listen, Pierce—ask her if a lot of people around her were sleeping."

"Sleeping? What's that got to do with anything?"

"Just a hunch. Something that I read along time ago just popped into my head, an old wives' tale from an aborigine tribe, I think."

"Harris, what the hell are you talking about?"

"Just ask the little girl and find out if the answer is yes. I might have a solution to the missing people."

Pierce thought Harris was losing it, but it wouldn't be the first time. After Amy was cleared by the doctor, she was taken back to Pierce. They both sat in the ER waiting room, eating some snacks. Pierce put her arm around Amy and asked her some more questions.

"Amy, I was just talking to Agent Harris and he asked me a funny question."

Amy was listening very carefully and tilted her head to the side and placed two fingers on her rosy cheeks…

"He wanted to know if the people around you were sleeping. You know, just before the crash…"

She thought real hard about it, trying to remember.

"I'm not sure…maybe…uhh…I think so…yeah…I'm pretty sure some of them were sleeping…"

Pierce called Harris back and relayed the answer.

"She's pretty sure that some of them were sleeping, but not her or her mother. Does that help you? "

"Well," Harris answered, "it just might. I've got to go and check something out. I'll meet you back at the motel in an hour. See if you can confirm the little girl's statement with her mother's—if you get a chance to talk to her." Before Pierce could tell Harris that the mother was unconscious, he hung up the phone and was gone.

Twenty minutes later officer Hunter came around the corner and told Pierce that Amy's mother was awake and the doctor said it was alright to go in and talk with her, as long as she doesn't get excited. Pierce smiled at Amy, and they both went in to the recovery room. Hunter was just ahead of them.

Alice Beckman was very nice. She confirmed that at least 15 to 20 people that were sitting around them were sleeping and that the only reason she wasn't sleeping was her nerves. Ann asked her a few more questions and then left Amy to reunite with her mother.

"All right officer Hunter, I'll see you in the morning for a full report. Oh, and listen, get some sleep, it's going to be another long day." Pierce smiled and left.

She met agent Harris back at the motel. It started raining hard again and she ran from her car to the room. He opened the door just as she reached it. Before she could get her coat off, Harris was holding his laptop under her nose, showing her the research information that he had found.

"Here it is in Ann," he said, "it was a study done on the Tonguehikin Tribe in the late 1800s, by Dr. H. Herman." Ann was trying to get her wet coat off as Harris continued. She interrupted him to run into the bathroom for a towel to dry her hair.

"So what does it say Harris, I don't have time to read it." she said as she exited the bathroom with a fluffy white towel wrapped around her hair.

"What Dr. Herman discovered was that if you die while you're sleeping, your conscious doesn't know that you're dead."

"…okay, Harris, but what's that got to do with the missing bodies and some ancient Indian tribe?" Ann was getting frustrated.

Harris took a breath before continuing, "Naturally when you die in your sleep from old age or a heart attack, you're probably by yourself, or with your spouse, and your state of mind is in an unconscious stage. When you're younger, however, and you're sleeping, happy and content, and then 'boom—you're dead…' The spirit isn't expecting to die, isn't ready. And so it reclaims the body. Those missing from the Silver Streak train didn't know they were dead, and so their spirits couldn't make the transition."

Pierce looked puzzled, Harris continued.

"So where did they go then? They certainly aren't at the crash site. And we also know…maybe…that they are not alive…they're not survivors. …so where are they?"

"Harris, what the hell are you talking about?"

"Listen Ann, look, just read this." Harris urged, while he

pulled out a piece of paper.

"What?" Pierce blurted out, getting annoyed and rolled her eyes.

"It's all right here Ann, just read this." Harris stated, pointing to the third paragraph on his copy page. ...

> *Tonight a small town in Deadwood, Missouri, reportedy was terrorized by ghost, or something of a spiritual nature. Local police are on their way to investigate the matter...*

"You have definitely lost it this time Harris. You mean to tell me that you think there is a connection between this train crash and ghost in a town in Missouri? Have you completely lost your mind?"

"I know how it sounds, but hear me out, Ann. It all fits together—mass killings, plus people in their sleep, equals... lost souls...you know...ghosts."

Ann burst out laughing.

"You mean zombies, ghouls, walking dead, Harris? Come on, now."

"Not zombies or walking dead. Just lost souls that don't realize they're dead."

"Okay, then. Why Missouri, Harris?"

"Tracks...the tracks. The railroad tracks, they go right by that town, well within two miles of that town. An Indian Tribe lived in that area over two hundred years ago." Harris said, as he walked over to his briefcase to grab more papers. "They were ancestors of the Tonguehikin's, and were massacred by some army soldiers while they were sleeping. Their spirits are said to still roam and haunt the area."

Pierce's mouth hung open in a slight smirk as she slowly removed the towel from her head.

"Ohh-kay. What do you want me to say here? You've totally lost your mind, Harris"

Harris just smiled and winked.

"Glad you're on board. I booked us on the next flight to St. Louis. It's about 90 miles from Deadwood."

Pierce was in disbelief.

"Did you get this authorized from Washington?"

"Not exactly. We'll think of an excuse on the way there."

Early the next morning they had breakfast with Hunter. Hunter informed them about the amount of cell phones that they found at the crash site, and that some of them were ringing. He wanted to know if he should answer them or wait for an official broadcast from the chief.

"That's a good question, Hunter," Pierce said. "What do you think Harris? What would you do?"

"Just to give them piece of mind, Hunter. Answer the phones, get the family information, then tell them you are still investigating the casualties, and as soon as you have positive ID's, you will personally contact them with an accurate update. That will give them some comfort, at least for now."

They said goodbye to Hunter and told him to keep them updated on any new information. Hunter also asked Harris to keep him in the loop from Missouri.

On the flight to Missouri, Harris continued to discuss his theory's with Pierce, and that this could be a ground breaking investigation.

"So what's your plan, Harris? Are you going to have a séance or something?"

"Good one, Ann. No, what I'm going to have is better than that. I have friends flying from New York to meet us. They're experts in supernatural phenomena."

"So those guys on that show 'Ghost Detectives?'"

"Ann, these gentlemen are the real McCoy. They know their stuff."

Ann laughed, and turned to look out the window.

When they landed at the St. Louis airport, Harris and Pierce were joined by the two "ghostbusters," Stu Phillips and Abe Goldsmith. After Harris did the introductions, they rented an SUV and drove out to Deadwood. The town looked like something out of the old west. There was a few run down houses, a bus station, gas station and a little diner. They pulled up to the pumps and tooted the horn.

"I'm going to fill her up," Harris said, "no telling how long and how far will have to go to find our missing 'passengers.' If anybody wants to stretch their legs, now's the time to do it."

Pierce got out and went inside in search of a rest room. Stu and Abe got out and walked to the back of the SUV to check their equipment.

Pierce noticed two old nickelodeons in the corner. They were dusty and scratched. She wondered if they still worked. Then she saw an old metal Greyhound bus sign hanging on the wall alongside two Esso gas signs. They were all pitted. They reminded her of her father's two car garage back home. The smell of lilacs filled the air, and then Pierce spotted the warm glow of a candle on the counter top, where a lady was ringing out a customer.

"Can I help you miss?" a sweet old lady asked from behind the counter.

She was wearing old faded bib overalls, a well-worn red and white plaid shirt, and a big smile on her well aged face.

"Yes you can—I was wondering if you had a ladies room?"

"Sure do, right over there sweetie." She answered, pointing

to the far corner of the store.

When Pierce came out of the ladies room, she chatted with the old lady, and bought some gum and a bottle of seven-up.

"I hear you had some excitement last night around here." Pierce said.

"Sure did." she answered, lighting up her corn-cob pipe, and taking a long drag on it. "It was awful," she leaned in towards Pierce, and blew the smoke out of the corner of he mouth, "ghosts, you know. We couldn't see 'em, but the dogs got hold of their scents and ran 'em out of town." She was starting to giggle now, and took another drag on her pipe, "It was a sight to see, sweetie. The menfolk got together and formed a search party. Then they started a-chasing them down the railroad tracks, you know…the spirts."

Pierce tilted her head, then asked, "How many of them were there?"

"I ain't sure, honey, but I can tell ya one thing—it was a lot more than one, and the law's up in the hills with the menfolk, chasing them scoundrels, right now. You ask a lot of questions sweetie—you ain't law, is ya?"

"Yes ma'am. I'm with the FBI." Pierce answered. Just then Harris walked in,

"You about ready to go, Pierce?"

"Yes, but before we go should we get some directions from this sweet old lady. She has a lot of information."

"Katie's my name." The old lady interrupted, and took another big drag on her pipe. "Where is it, you wanna go?"

"Well," Harris answered, "we would like to find the location of that little town where all the trouble was last night."

"Oh, you mean Coal Town. That's easy—just go back out towards the railroad tracks, follow them down, 'bout four miles, just west of here. There's a dirt road that runs along the railroad bed, all the way down to the foothills. Can't miss 'em—the law's been driving out there almost all day now." Katie tapped her pipe on the counter and knocked out all the burnt tobacco, and smiled at Pierce.

"Thank you very much, Katie," Piece said, smiling, then heading for the door.

"Ya'll come back on your way back through!"

Pierce noticed that Katie had a twinkle in her big brown eyes as she waved good bye.

They all jumped in the SUV and headed west, following Katie's directions. The service road paralleled the railroad tracks for four miles. That's when they reached an area with a lean-to, where there was approximately fifteen lawmen and ten civilians, standing around and arguing about something.

Harris and Pierce were the first to approach the group, while Abe and Stu unloaded their equipment.

"How you doing, Sheriff?" Harris said as they approached. The sheriff turned around, looking frustrated as Harris continued, "FBI. I'm Agent Harris, and this is Agent Pierce. We're tracking some missing passengers from the train wreck."

"What train wreck?" The sheriff asked, "what the hell are you talking about?"

That caught Harris off guard before he realized that they couldn't see the passengers or anything that looked like a train wreck. They all looked at Harris like he was from Mars. Harris wasn't sure what to say now, so he asked them if they would mind if he looked around.

"Harris, what train wreck?" Pierce asked, under her breath. Harris walked away over towards the lean-to, Pierce followed close behind.

"What's going on Harris?"

"Don't you get it Ann? How do you think they got all the way out here?"

"Who?"

"The missing people from the train crash in PA? They're here, or at least I think it's them—who else could it be?"

Ann was totally confused again, but that wasn't anything new for her, working with Harris. An old man walked over to Harris. He looked like he was at least eighty. He was wearing a worn-out camouflage jacket, with tattered jeans and hunting boots. He got really close to Harris then nudged him. The old buck grinned at Harris, his wrinkled face was covered with white whiskers, that were stained by tobacco juice.

"You mean ghost, doncha?" the old man whispered.

Harris nodded.

"Well, I couldn't see 'em…but my hound could…and I'm tellin' ya, they are here." His smile grew broader. He had the same twinkle in his eyes that Katie had.

"Head up that there way if yer a-looking for them ghosts." he said, pointing up at the mountainside. "First we chased them outta town, then we lost 'em for awhile. They camped here for a little while last night, as much as I can tell, then we chased 'em up into the hills. We never got a good look at 'em, and the law thinks we're all crazy." Just then a large State Trooper walked over and butted into the conversation.

"Don't listen to this old coot or his buddies. The whole town called 911 last night stating that their town was being attached by terrorists, and they've had us out here all night looking for ghosts. Can you believe that shit?"

"What makes you think they're not telling the truth?" Harris asked.

"I deal in facts." the trooper said, "and I'm telling you, they should all be committed." He walked away pissed off and told his men to wrap it up. The old man whispered to Harris again.

"The evidence is all over the place—follow me and I'll show ya."

They tagged along with the old guy until he stopped. "Right

here, in this here area, you will see three or four campfires. And check out all the footprints—they're all over the place!" The old buck was getting excited. He spit some tobacco juice out and it almost hit Harris's shoe. "The best we can figure, there's 'bout 30 or 40 of 'em altogether."

Harris looked at all the foot prints. The guy was right. He walked around, slowly looking at empty water bottles, soda cans and various food wrappers.

"As far as I know, ghost don't eat or drink anything—if there is a such thing as a ghost, anyway." Pierce said. Harris didn't answer her. Stu and Abe were lost for words. But not Harris.

"Where are the westbound tracks?" Harris asked the old guy.

"About forty yards in that direction." He answered, pointing to a small ridge behind the lean-to. They followed Harris as he walked in that direction towards the tracks. He picked up a trail of footprints walking west on the railroad tracks. They followed them for five minutes or so, until they came upon the twisted railroad tracks. A little farther up, they found several more pairs of footprints and Harris tried to figure out what had happened here.

They returned back to the campsite, where the old guy said goodbye and rejoined his buddies. Stu and Abe got their equipment set up and were walking around filming the area by the lean-to. Pierce and Harris walked over to them.

"Hey guys, getting anything yet?"

"You won't believe this Ted. All of our gauges are topping off the charts!" Abe announced. "There must be a hundred spirits around here!"

"More like forty-something." Harris replied.

"So what now Harris?" Pierce said, "you've seemed to hit the nail on the head with your theory about this whole thing. What's your next move?"

"I'm not sure Ann, I'm happy just to find them…or even

traces of them."

"Hey guys—let's go set up where the tracks end from the east, and see what we find over there."

"Sound good, Harris. Give us a couple of minutes."

By the time Stu and Abe moved everything, most of the police were gone. Two or three of them stayed behind to keep pedestrians away.

"Ted, you're going want to see this! It's amazing!" Abe was peering into the lens of his special camera.

"Whatcha ya got buddy?"

"Take a look!" Harris couldn't believe his eyes. There it was, as big as day—The Ghost Train. *The Silver Streak,* just like the one in Pennsylvania. *Exactly* like the one in Pennsylvania. It was tipped on its side, burrowed into the dirt. Small traces of smoke were still escaping from its broken windows.

"Holy shit! I can't believe it! Do you believe it, Abe?"

"No...no, this is impossible Ted...it just can't be..."

Harris called Pierce over, then Pierce and Stu took their turns looking at it. Pierce got a little faint. She sat down for a few minutes, to compose herself.

"Well guys," Harris started, "are you ready to find proof of the passengers, whether they're dead or alive or even if they are real spirits?"

"You bet your ass that we are ready to go! Give us a couple minutes to round up all of our equipment."

"Pierce, you okay?"

"I think I'm in total shock. Pinch me to make sure I'm not dreaming."

While the guys were packing up their equipment, Harris took the opportunity to talk to one of officers and find out if he would be their guide. He informed him that there was a very good trail leading up the mountain and that's the way the first search party went. Ann went back to the car, got her backpack, put on her hiking boots, and grabbed a few bottles of water.

"We're ready to roll, Ted. We have everything we need. Right, Stu?" Abe asked.

"Yep, let's go find them." Stu confirmed. They started up the mountain trail, without knowing what lie ahead of them.

After walking for hours, Dan and the group finally made it to the summit of the mountain. They all sat down and took a well-deserved break.

"Looks like they gave up, Dan." Eli stated, looking back down the trail.

"Yah, looks that way," Dan replied, "and it's about time. Speaking of time, what time do you think it is?"

"I'd say around noon." Sally cut in, holding her hand up over her eyebrow while squinting at the sun. "It's a beautiful day, isn't it, Jimmy?"

"It sure is, mom," he replied, "Dan, when can we get something to eat? You never did bring me anything back last night like you promised. "

"I know Jimmy. Things didn't go the way I planned. "

"Dan," Hank said, "some people are leaving—said they are tired of running. Their going down a pathway, that they've found over there, behind that outcropping of rock." Dan turned in the direction that Hank was pointing towards. He watched them slowly descend down a trail, heading westward.

"Where do you think their going?"

"Beats me Hank. I hope they have better luck than we had last night. We'll wait here for a little while, I'm sure all those cops and those wacky old bastards have gone home by now.

It's been hours and we haven't seen a sign of them."

"And we're all starving too," Jimmy groaned.

"I guess we could head back to the train. Maybe there's something we missed inside. Food, water, anything. Then we'll take the tracks east, the way Joe Rogers went. They never came back, maybe they found something." They rested for two hours and then started back down the mountain trail.

"Hold up," Dan said softly, "look guys, three or four people are coming up the trail." Eli and Hank turned and stared down the trail along with Dan.

"The two in the front look like cops," Eli stated, "but those other two are—I don't know—carrying some kind of equipment. Let's go down and talk to them. What do you say, Dan?"

"All right Eli. I'm getting sick of running away, too." Dan said, then walked over to the others and explained their plan.

Hellen said that she would like to go with them, explaining that having a women along would be beneficial. Hellen asked Hank to keep an eye on Bernie for her. So Dan, Eli and Hellen made their way down the trail, while Hank and the others stayed behind.

They were gone less than five minutes when David Cummings showed up, with two bags of food and drinks, for everybody in the group.

"Hi everybody," David said, "dig in, eat all you want. There's plenty more where this came from. Where's Dan?" Everybody except for Hank swarmed David and dug into the bags of food.

"Where did you get all of the stuff, mister?" Jimmy asked.

"I found it on the trail over there," David answered, pointing to the West Trail." And you don't have to call me 'mister,' Jimmy, you can call me Dave. Okay?"

Jimmy nodded as he stuffed food in his mouth.

"Eat up everybody! Plenty more! Plenty! Also, I found a nice town over there. There's a motel, a burger shops, and

I assume workign telephones. It seems like a great place to lie low, maybe even relax while we make calls to everyone back home."

"Let's go there now!" Jimmy exclaimed.

Everyone let out a cheer, and finished eating while they gathered their belongings. Not too long after they were following David down the trail. Hank held back, hoping Dan and the rest would catch up soon.

"What about Dan and the others?" Sally inquired.

"Ah, don't worry. They'll catch up." David answered back.

"I'll wait for them." Jerry Cooper offered.

"Don't be silly Jerry," David countered, "you need to stay with your sister. Let's leave them a note or something."

"I don't mind waiting here for them." Jerry insisted.

David was getting annoyed. He leaned into Jerry, and whispered in his ear,

"You're coming with us, son. Let's go. You don't want the others to find out about your sexual exploits with daddy, do you?"

Jerry stopped dead in his tracks, his insides twisted instantly. He was in disbelief. He looked over at Patti. She was smiling and happy. He wanted to say something to her, but his mind drew a blank. Somehow, this son of a bitch *knew*. But how? He thought he was going to throw up. Reluctantly, he followed David and the others down the trail. Hank tried to get to Jerry, but he was too far ahead of him, and David was blocking the trail.

––––––––––––––

Dan, Eli, and Hellen met the FBI team halfway down the hill. They stopped ten feet short of the team. Pierce and Harris continued to move towards them.

"STOP!" Stu warned. He had his infrared camera pointed right at Dan and the others. "They're here! Standing right in front of us!" He was almost giddy.

Pierce and Harris we're looking straight ahead. They didn't see anything. Harris even tried squinting with his hand on his brow to block the sun.

"Holy shit!" Abe shouted, peering into the camera. He started waving at the three of them. "Hello…ahhh, how are you?…oh, I guess that's a stupid question since you're dead. Sorry."

"What the hell is this guy's problem?" Eli asked. Dan shrugged his shoulders, he was totally confused. Just then, Hellen stepped up to the plate,

"Hi, my name is Hellen Higgins, and this is Dan and Eli. We were in the train crash." No response from any of them.

Hellen turned to Dan and asked, "Why aren't they answering me?" She turn back towards the four of them, "Can't you hear me!" She cried out in an frazzled voice.

Harris and Pierce waited impatiently wondering why Abe stopped them from continuing along the trail. Abe handed the camera back to Stu, then he walked in front of Harris and Pierce.

"Bear with me, Ted. Just trust me. Give me a minute and you will understand."

With that, he turned back towards Hellen and raised his hands up in a gesture of friendship. Then, very slowly, and distinctly he asked, "Can you hear me?"

"Of course we can hear you! We're standing right in front of you! Why the hell *wouldn't* we hear you!" Dan answered. He was beyond angry by now. Hellen grabbed his arm and told him to calm down. Eli was beginning to understand.

"Don't you understand Dan," Hellen explained, "we can hear them, but they can't hear us."

"Get the spectrum frequency meter out of the backpack, Stu!" Abe excitedly ordered.

Stu pulled out the SFM and almost dropped it on the ground—his adrenaline was in high gear. He managed to turn it on and pointed it in the direction of Dan and the others. Again, Abe instructed Hellen to say something,

"Just keep talking and I will see if I can get a reading on you." Abe kept watching Hellen through the camera while instructing Stu to fine tune the SFM.

"Eli," Dan asked, "am I going crazy? Or are you just as confused at this bullshit as I am?"

"Give it a chance. I think Hellen is on to something."

Hellen continued talking to Abe. Dan was ready to explode.

"I GOT HER!" Stu announced, and shared the monitor with Abe, who was ecstatic by now. "Listen! We got them! I can hear them. It's not super clear—kinda like a tape in slow motion—but we got them!"

"That's great!" Abe said. "We can start communicating with them. Agent Harris, we're good to go. Ask them direct questions and we'll see what happens."

"Are you sure that your equipment is accurate?"

Abe nodded "I'm positive." Then he turned and looked at Hellen. He raised his arm up, and pointed his index finger towards her, "I can hear you. Give me one minute to explain the situation to Agent Harris."

Hellen was relieved, and tried to calm Dan down and gave him a big hug. Then she hugged Eli. "Isn't this wonderful, they can hear us now!" Eli nodded, but Dan was still confused.

Understanding the situation, Harris started, "First of all, let me introduce myself and the others. I'm Agent Ted Harris. This is Agent Ann Pierce. The guy behind the camera is Stu Phillips, and Dr. Abe Goldsmith is our science consultant."

Eli introduced himself, Hellen and Dan.

"Let me try explain what is going on here," Harris continued, "I have been investigating this train wreck from the beginning, and I'll be as brief as I can, though this may take awhile." Everybody sat down and got comfortable. Stu made sure to keep the SFM on them and recorded.

"The first thing I want to get across to everybody is that you will probably not believe what I'm about to explain. The real train crash happened in Pennsylvania, just east of Pittsburgh, in a little town called, Kurtzville." He explained to them about the train trestle exploding, possibly by a terrorist, and he also told them about the missing passengers and casualties. Then he explained his research of that old Indian tribe. Dan had heard enough, his head was spinning and he was pissed, he vaulted off the ground and shouted.

"So what the fuck are you saying!? That we're dead!? We're ghosts!?"

"Calm down Dan!" Eli said, "you're getting all worked up."

"Is this guy for real? Do you believe this shit? I don't know what's going on here, but I know one thing…I'm not dead, and neither are you two!"

"Dan," Hellen cried out, "calm down and think about what Agent Harris is trying to tell us. First of all, he's telling us that the train didn't crash here, and that would account for the missing people here."

"Yes, but you also heard him say that they have missing people up in PA, too. And for another thing, why can't they see us? They can hear us now, right?" Hellen wasn't sure about anything right now, except that Abe was trying his hardest to communicate with them. Agent Harris asked Stu if there were any other traces of people on his camera.

"Ah, no, I don't see anybody else. That's what I have, just three of them."

"Where are the rest of people from the accident?" Harris asked them.

"I don't know about you two," Dan said, "but I've had

enough of this shit. I'm leaving and going back to the others."
Dan stood up, turned and walked away, leaving Eli and Hellen
sitting there.

"Come on, Dan. Just hear these guys out." Eli said. "What
can it hurt?"

Dan kept walking. Hellen wanted to go with Dan. She
felt a connection with him but she also wanted answers from
Agent Harris.

"Hey Abe," Stu commented, peering into his camera screen,
"One of them is walking away. He's walking back up the path."

"Which one is it?" Harris asked, walking over to Stu and
looked into the screen. Stu pointed out the movement to
Harris on his screen, and they both watched Dan go up the
path. Abe started picking up more static and noise—it was
Hellen asking something.

"Ted," Abe said, "I think the lady wants some
more information."

"Agent Harris," Hellen said, "can you give us more details
on exactly what happened?"

"Hellen," he started off slowly, "the thing of it is, all of
you, all the people in your group—forty, maybe forty five of
you—I'm not sure of the exact amount, but you all passed away
back in PA. I know it's hard to comprehend that. You have to
try to understand, why this happened." He could see Hellen
shivering and tears started to run down her cheeks. "Do you
understand what I'm saying?"

"I think so," Hellen confirmed. She turned to Eli, "Do you
think he is right?"

He thought about it for awhile, then shook his head slowly.
"I don't feel dead."

"Eli," she asked in a low tone, "are you hungry?"

"What are you talking about? Why are you asking me that?"

"Because Eli…I'm not really hungry anymore, and neither

are you. None of us are hungry, we just think we are because it's a habit, embedded in our heads." A warm feeling overcame Hellen, "We …are …dead." Tears were streaming down her face. The feeling intensified, and she began to feel wonderful. She was at peace with herself, and smiled, "Eli, it's going to be okay. It's going to be, fine."

Hellen looked up at the sky. It was crystal blue with white puffy clouds. She felt like a little girl again, skipping down a garden path in the springtime, smelling fresh blooming lilacs, and feeling the warmth of the sun, shining down on her shoulders and arms. Her body started tingling with a feeling of assurance.

"Goodbye Eli. I'll see you soon." Hellen's soul slowly lifted up and gently rotated in the air. After a few moments, she ascended it into the sky, leaving a spiral trail of sparkling remnants.

Eli looked on in disbelief. He was all choked up. Then he felt a tingling in his chest. He stood up and raised his hands to the sky, "Take me father! I'm ready to go." His feet raised off the sweet, green grass, and he twisted to the left and spun up to touch the sky. In an instant, he was gone, too.

They couldn't see Hellen or Eli now. Harris was on his feet, looking straight up in disbelif, then he looked in the direction of Abe and Stu. They were totally mystified.

"Holy shit!" Abe exclaimed, "They're gone! You did it, Harris—you set them free!" Stu agreed then looked back to his monitor. All that was left on the screen was faint, dying embers laying on the dusty trail.

Pierce looked up at the sky. She held her hands out, attempting to catch some of the falling fragments of Hellen and Eli. She could swear that she smelled lilacs. After a long moment, they all tried to compose themselves.

"How are we going to write up this report, Harris?" Pierce

asked. "No proof, no witnesses. They will put us in a padded cell and throw away the key if they ever knew that we were out here, especially with the 'Ghostbusters.'"

"Well, people," Harris said smiling, "you have just witnessed a little known phenomenon called *'Souls rising to heaven,'* which the human mind doesn't have the capability of processing, even though you've just witnessed it with your own two eyes."

"What the hell are you talking about Harris?" Pierce disputed, "we all know just what happened." Abe and Stu were bewildered, but nodded their heads in agreement.

"You see, Pierce," Harris said, shaking his head, "they don't believe it. Now, if they saw it on TV, or in a movie, they wouldn't think anything of it, but…"

"But nothing Harris, let's go after the other guy. You know…Don…Dan…whatever his name was…and get to the bottom of this crazy case so I can get back to reality."

Harris agreed with her. The he looked her in the eye s and asked,

"But, it was beautiful, wasn't it? It was just…beautiful"

They started gathering their equipment and backpacks. Stu looked into the viewfinder one last time to make certain that no one was on the pathway.

CHAPTER 6

AND BACK AT HOME

Clara Dawson couldn't believe what she was watching on the television set.

"Breaking News! There has been a horrific train crash in western Pennsylvania, just east of Pittsburgh. It's been reported that there are over twenty casualties. Stay tuned for live coverage at the scene!"

Oh my God—Phil! Clara headed for the phone in the kitchen and dialed Phil's cell phone…no answer. *He always answers me…* She tried again and again…then she called her sister…

"Wendy, did you hear the news yet?"

"Yes, I just saw it. How's Phil?"

"I don't know, he's not answering his phone." Clara broke down and began to sob uncontrollably.

"Calm down, sis. That doesn't mean anything. He could have just dropped his phone." Wendy was worried for her sister, "Just try to keep calm sis, I'll be right over."

Jimmy didn't show up for school and his home room

teacher noted in her daily log. At recess time she went to the office and handed in her report. The secretary made her usual calls to all the absentee kid's parents, as required by school policy. Most of the parents answered and gave the usual excuses, with the exception of two: Jimmy and another kid.

The secretary made the call to the authorities about the other kid, noting the close proximity to Jimmy's home. In the afternoon, they begrudgingly drove out to do their duty. After stopping at the other kid's house and reaming out his drunken father, threatening to arrest him for not knowing where his son was, they decided to check out Jimmy's house. They called the school for his address and headed over for a look.

When they approached Jimmy's house, the first thing they noticed was the door was ajar. Cautiously, they moved on to the porch and yelled in. Nothing.

"Police—anybody home?" They instinctively drew their weapons and stood on either side of the door. "Police! Please come to the door!" They entered and began their search, room by room.

———

Patti and Jerry's parents got up at their usual time of 10 a.m. Their father hadn't worked for years thanks to a fake back injury. He collected a hefty monthly paycheck from disability. His wife Barb worked second shift at a local doughnut shop. They headed to the kitchen for coffee and toast, kicked on the TV and started to read the paper. At 11 o'clock the phone rang. The school principal informed them that neither Jerry nor Patti, showed up for school.

"Little bastards…where the hell could they be?"

"Who, George?"

"Patti and Jerry. They didn't go to school today."

"That's strange. They love school."

"Well, I'm going to get to the bottom of this. I'm going to look for them, and when I catch them, they'll be sorry."

Approx. 8 a.m., west coast time.

"Mom, turn on the news!" Lisa shouted out to her mother, who was making breakfast.

"Why, what's up?"

"Just do it mom, please!"

Jan reluctantly turned on the kitchen TV. She preferred quiet mornings and hot coffee.

"Oh my God! That's the train that grandpa's on!" She grabbed her phone and hit speed dial. Static.

"Hello—Dad, are you alright?"

More static.

"Daddy!...Dad, can you hear me!...Dad..."

They both stared at the news, taking in every detail.

"Call your father and your sister."

"But she's in class, mom."

"I don't care. I want them both here."

Wendy arrived at Clara's within the hour. She tried to comport herself as best she could.

"I tried calling him again sis, but nothing. What am I going to do?"

"Stay calm, sweetie. If something's wrong, I'm sure someone will call."

They watch the news all day, their hopes got a little better when the news stated that some of the passengers were missing.

"Ya see sis, there's a good chance Phil's alive, he probably just wander off from the wreck, so stay positive..." After three days, and hundreds of phone calls, Clara was giving up hope.

Tons of friends and neighbors were stopping by with food and good wishes. Her neighbor, Doreen, stopped by with a meatloaf, and cornered Clara in the kitchen.

"How you holding up, Clare? You doing okay?"

"I guess. I just wish someone would call and let me know one way or the other."

"I know how you feel sweetheart, listen…" Doreen leaned in, real close, "I might know someone that could help…"

"Oh my goodess—who?"

"Well, it's a little bit unorthodox, but I have this aunt, and she has this—*sort of gift*—if you know what I mean…"

"Really, Doreen?" Clara whispered, "and you think she could really help?"

"I know she can, I've seen her do it a hundred times. I can call her, if you like."

———————————

The police didn't find anything on the first or second floors. They carefully descended the basement steps, guns in hand and flashlights on. That's when they discovered the body of Sally's husband.

"Holy shit Rick—look at this!"

"Oh man, what happened to this poor guy?" After eight hours of police investigation, the detectives decided that they needed to talk to Sally Weeks and her son. The only question was: where the hell were they? They put out a BOLO and all the other means to find them. The next day they got a hit from the video cameras at the train station.

"You gotta be kidding. They were on that train?"

"Looks that way. So they're either dead or missing, right? We're never going to close the file on this one…"

———————————

The longer George Cooper looked for Patti and Jerry, the more pissed off he got. That's when he started to realize if they told anybody about him, he was going to jail. He had to find them and he had to find them fast.

His wife waited at home thinking about her kids, knowing the awful secret all these years. Why did she let it go on? And now, they were gone…didn't even leave a note… She hated herself and she hated her so-called husband even more. She wanted to curl up into a ball and die.

Jan kept calling her dad, crying her eyes out. Her husband came home early from work and ran into the living room. The first thing he noticed was that both of his daughter's were sitting next to their mother on the couch, with their arms around her.

"Don't worry, mom. He's going to be alright. He's a tough guy."

Nothing they could say or do helped her right now. She just kept calling and crying.

The table was set in Clara's dining room exactly the way Doreen instructed. Clara took the leafs out of the table, making it round. She placed her best lace table cloth on the table, the one that her mother gave her many years ago. Three white candles were placed in silver candlestick holders, and were set in the center of the table, one foot apart, from the other. The aroma of freshly brewed coffee mixed with freshly baked chocolate cake filled the entire house. Six chairs were evenly placed around the table. The light on the front porch and the light in the kitchen were the only ones left on. Wendy sat in the kitchen nervously sipping her coffee, wondering if this idea was a healthy thing for Clara. The doorbell chimed.

Four women enter the house, all dressed in black. One wore a veil, concealing her face. Doreen made the introductions. Clara heard the names, smiled politely, but instantly forgot them. They sat down on the dining room chairs according to the instructions from the veil lady. She had a thick accent—*old school Italian*, Wendy thought.

She pulled some objects out of her hand bag, laid them in front of her, then mumbled something—maybe a prayer. Doreen told them to join hands and not to say word during the ceremony. Then it commenced. Mumbling, swaying back and forth, praying, shouting, crying. Soon the candles started to flicker, hands clenched tightly.

"Phil...Phil," the old lady whispered. Clara felt faint. Wendy held her hand and caressed it with her thumb. Slowly the old lady looked up at Clara.

"He is here, Clara. He says he's sorry, and that loves you very much, but won't be returning."

"No...no...Phil. That can't be. You promised you'd never leave me all alone...it just can't be." Clara's face was getting pale. Wendy wanted to stop this whole thing. She didn't believe this whole stunt anyway.

"...this whole thing is a lie!" Clara announced, "Ask him what the combination is for the safe!"

The old lady got annoyed, and Doreen looked offended. The other two ladies just stared at Clara.

"R-21, L-14, R-27"

Clara passed out.

George Cooper finally got home at midnight. Barb was still curled up on the floor, next to the couch.

"Those ungrateful bastards—can't find them anywhere."

George said, then focused sharply on Barb, "What the hell are you doing? Aren't you suppose to be working?"

She didn't lift her head up. She just laid there, not acknowledging him at all, wanting to die.

"I'll try again tomorrow, maybe I'll have better luck then. I'm going to bed, you coming?"

Barb said nothing.

"Suit yourself, bitch."

An hour later, while George was sleeping, Barb shot him in the head, then turned the gun on herself.

Dan Jensen's daughter wasn't giving up. She continued calling her father every 15 minutes. On the third day, he finally answered his phone. Nobody was at home to verify her communication with him, but in her heart, she knew it was her father.

"Daddy! Are you alright?"

…static…

"Daddy can you hear me!"

"Jen…static…hardly…hear…you…"

"DADDY!…" The line dropped.

When her husband and the girls arrived home from the store she told them about the phone call. They didn't know what to believe. They tried to be sympathetic, but they had their doubts. She didn't want to get into an argument about it, but she knew in her heart what she had heard. She knew he wasn't dead and that someday he would show up at her front door and give her a big hug and kiss.

Chapter 7

Lost Souls

Dan followed the trail to the top of the mountain, where he left everyone that morning. It was a long uphill walk and he was feeling burnt out. He got to the spot where they were supposed to be. Or at least he thought it was where he left them. He scanned the surrounding area, and even crawled up on a boulder to look around. The sun was bright, so he shielded his eyes with his hands on his forehead. No sign of them at all.

He jumped down off of the boulder and checked for footprints in the dirt and sand. They lead to the east trail, so he headed down the trail in search of them. He walked for a good hour before he heard some people laughing and talking. As he rounded a bend in the trail, he spotted an off-white rundown motel with green shutters and a worn-out green shingled roof. It had a large front porch with a hanging swing, which connected to the porch ceiling with two old rusted chains. Next to the motel was an abandoned gas station. The gas pumps were rusted with faded out green and white paint—they looked like they were from the fifties. There was an old "Sinclare" sign barely attached to the face of the building. The overhead door was halfway opened, and most of the windows were busted out or cracked.

Dan spotted Jimmy running and laughing loudly. It reminded him of the other day—when he first met Jimmy running around the train platform. It was just a few short days ago, but it seemed like an eternity.

"Jimmy!" Dan hollered and waved at him.

Jimmy ran over and threw his arms around Dan.

"How you doing buddy, how are you?"

"Great Dan!" He answered, and continued hugging him. "I missed you a lot, where ya been?"

Before Dan could answer, Jimmy shouted out...

"Wanna go on over there? We have tons of food and soda and everything!" Dan smiled and walked over with him towards the motel, wondering where they got all the food and drinks. Jimmy took Dan's big hand in his, and led him into the motel.

Everyone was there: Sally, Jerry and Patti Cooper, Bernie and the rest. They greeted Dan with a warm welcome. He was wondering where Hank was. Out of the corner of his eye, he spotted Dave Cummings and got that familiar twinge on the back of his neck. He sure as hell didn't like that guy and was wondering where the hell he was for the past two days.

"Hey Danny Boy," David said, smiling, and holding out his hand for a shake. "How are you big guy? Where ya been?" Dan reluctantly shook his hand—it was cold and clammy, and sent a chill up Dan's spine.

"Hello David. What are you up to? I haven't seen you since the other night."

This was the first time that he actually got a good look at David. His face was rugged, sported a few small scars, but was clean shaven. That's what puzzled Dan: how the hell he was clean shaven.

"I know Dan, I've been real busy. I went looking for the first rescue team. You know, the one that Joe Rogers headed up. Couldn't find them at all. It was like they disappeared—just vanished off the face of the earth. It was the strangest thing, ya know? Then I stumbled onto this oasis in the middle of nowhere. Good thing, too, because your people were starving to death. I guess you didn't have much luck finding help or food or anything, huh?" He was really rubbing it into Dan's face, and Dan was getting pissed.

"Well, I guess I don't have your sense of finding things, or not finding things, as you mentioned. You know, Joe's search team—just how far did you go down the tracks? You couldn't have been too far, if you're back here already." Dan was giving it right back to David, and really enjoying it.

David was grinding his teeth. He wanted to pound Dan into the ground, right where he stood, but he knew better, and kept cool.

"Listen Danny Boy, at least your people are smiling and happy now." David bragged, looking over at the lost souls, who were filling up their bellies with his free offerings. Soon, he thought, they would be *ripe…*

"No, *Davey Boy*, you listen. Where did this food come from?"

Before Dave could respond, Jimmy interrupted, "Dan wanna play catch with me?"

"Sure Jimmy, I'd love to." Dan stood up, giving David a snide look. He unclenched his fist and walked off to play catch with Jimmy.

I've got to get rid of that bastard, David whispered to himself, *before he ruins all of my plans…*

Sally weeks spotted Dan playing catch with Jimmy and walked over to say hello. "Where did the two of you find that dirty old baseball? It looks like it was washed up from a flood." They all laughed and Dan gave her a big smile.

"I got it over there mom," Jimmy declared, pointing under the porch of the motel. "It works good, mom—see?" He tossed the ball at her. "Catch it mom!"

She jumped to the side, and kept her hands away from the dirty ball. "I'm not catching that germ-infested thing," she jokingly said as she walked over to Dan. "Dan, when you're finished playing mudball with Jimmy, can I have a talk with you?"

"Sure, no problem. See you in a little while. Oh, by the way, where's Hank?"

"He left earlier to scout around for more survivors—said he would be back by dark."

Jimmy and Dan played catch for another twenty minutes and Dan suggested they get something to drink. The sun was like a big, red ball sinking in the sky, with purple and orange wispy clouds sliding in front of it.

"Isn't that a beautiful sunset, Dan?" Sally asked as she sat down on the porch swing of the old motel.

"Yeah, it really is. I never get tired of looking at sunsets and billowy white clouds in a clear blue sky. They have a soothing effect on me. Good for my stress, they tell me. So how are you holding up?"

"Pretty good I guess, considering this whole wild adventure. Dan I've got a question for you."

"Go ahead, shoot."

"What do you think of that David guy?"

Dan scratched his head, then looked back at Sally. "I don't like him at all. I don't trust him. I think he is hiding something, and I get a bad feeling in my gut every time I see him."

"Me neither. He gives me the creeps and he upset Jerry Cooper this morning—got him real upset."

"Oh? How did that happen?"

"I'm not sure. I think he whispered something in Jerry's ear when Jerry wanted to wait for you on the trail. Whatever he said to him got Jerry really upset. He hasn't talked to anyone since then—not even his sister. I was wondering if you could talk to him and find out what's wrong."

"Sure,where he's at?"

"I'm not sure where he got off too. You'll have to look for him."

Dan found Jerry sitting by himself, leaning against an oak tree in front of the old gas station. He looked distraught and was reading a book.

"Hey Jere. How are you making out?"

"Oh, hi Dan. Okay I guess, I'm just a little tired."

"Where's your sister?"

"I think she's over at the motel with the others. She's feeling a little low."

"Why's that?"

"She's been having bad dreams every night since we got on the train back in New York City"

"I'm sorry to hear that. Is everything OK with you? You look a little depressed."

"Naw, I'm alright, but I'm a little pissed off at that David guy. He gives me the creeps, and I just don't trust him. And you know another thing Dan, I don't remember seeing him on the train, before or after the wreck."

Jerry was right about that one, Dan thought, he didn't remember seeing David either and had no idea where he came from on the night of the crash.

"By the way Dan, where are Hellen and Eli?"

"They decided to stay back and talk to the FBI and some news reporters. Real strange ones. They had all this strange looking equipment and kept asking all these bizarre questions about sleeping and dying. Oh, and something about the first train wreck? I couldn't make heads or tails out of the whole discussion. They said they couldn't see us, but I could see them.

Then Hellen asked me to have patience and to keep quiet and listen. She went right on talking to one of them. I thought it was a bunch of bullshit, and I got pissed off, so I left them there, talking their asses off."

"They didn't go with you?"

"Nope, I don't know where they are now, or what they're doing."

"DAN," Sally broke in…"Jimmy is gone and I don't know where he is! One minute he was playing tag with some kids and the next minute he was gone! I looked all over for him but didn't have any luck."

"All right calm down Sally, where did you see him last?"

"Well, at first they were in front of the motel, running and laughing, then they were running around that old tire swing," she said, as she pointed to the big tree in front of the motel. "and then I saw them go in between those old gas pumps, right over there."

"Jerry would you mind looking over by the garage and around the pumps? I'll go around the back of the motel and the garage. Sally, you go inside the motel, check the kitchen area and the bathrooms too. I'm sure somebody has seen him. Oh, ask the kids that he was playing with if they know where he might be."

They all took off in their separate directions. Dan thought for sure that Jimmy would show up in a couple of minutes. After twenty minutes, Sally was getting freaked out. It was totally dark by now and Dan knew that Jimmy would've never left alone. He was thinking that somebody had to take him.

David Cummings! It had to be him.

"I'll kill that bastard!"

Dan headed back to the motel and burst through the door, then looked all around.

"Cummings! Where is David Cummings? Anybody see

him? " People started shaking their heads, five or six of them yelled out, no.

"I saw him 45 minutes ago." Bernie yelled out, "outside on the porch swing."

"Me too." Somebody added.

"What's all the hollering about?" A voice from the back of the room shouted out. Everyone turned around. It was David Cummings, standing in the doorway of the kitchen. "What's going on? You're yelling loud enough to wake up the dead." he said with a big smirk on his face.

"Where in the hell have you been, Cummings?" Dan demanded.

"I just stepped outside five minutes ago to take a piss, ah,pardon my French ladies," he chuckled, "so what's all the commotion about?"

"Jimmy's been missing for over an hour now!" Sally broke in.

"Well, I just saw him out back, with his buddies, catching fireflies a minute ago. I walked right passed them."

"That's bullshit, I was just out there looking for him." Dan yelled.

"Well, let's form a search party and go look for him." David snickered.

"We have been looking for him," Dan snarled, "I'm going to ask you again—where have you been for the last hour? It sure as hell doesn't take an hour to take a piss."

Dan knew this prick was behind the whole thing. Somehow, he would prove it. Most of the people helped search, while a few of the wounded people stayed behind in the motel. Bernice told Sally that she would stay behind and tend to their needs.

Dan, Sally, Patti and Jerry started off in one direction looking for Jimmy. They continued searching together but slowly spread out looking here and there. In the distance

Patti saw that David's group had made torches and also had a few flashlights. She wondered how they made the torches so quickly, since according to David he had just found out that Jimmy was missing.

Dan searched through some old rusted cars and trucks. He thought Sally was close by, but when he backed out of an old Chevy pick up truck, he felt a nasty chill go down the back of his neck, just like before, on the train.

"Jimmy! Jimmy!" he yelled out, "Can you hear me!" He stood up straight and scanned the whole area. He saw a bunch of fireflies whizzing around, and he could hear the sound of katydids chirping, except this time, it sounded like they were calling out Jimmy's name.

David Cummings managed to sneak Sally away from the search party, by showing her a piece of Jimmy's torn shirt. He told her that he had just found it on a narrow pathway, a couple hundred feet from them.

Sally quickly followed David down the path without any hesitation…A pathway…that she would never return on…

"How far do we have to go?" Sally asked as she trudged along.

"Just a little further down this pathway." David said, pointing towards some large rocks. "Right down there. Yes, that's it—right over there is where I found the torn piece of Jimmy's shirt. He can't be far now."

"Jimmy! Jimmy! It's mommy, sweetheart, where are you?"

"You know Sally," David hissed "I know who you really are."

Sally stopped dead in her tracks. She turned and looked at David. He looked different to her now. His cheeks were drawn in tight. His eyes seemed to glow in the darkness. He had a beastly look about him, and his grin sent chills up her spine.

"What are you talking about?" She said, gritting her teeth.

"I know that you killed your husband, and I know you lied to your little boy." he hissed, "and I also know…you sure as hell…CAN NEVER GO BACK HOME AGAIN!" By this time, David was in a full satanic rage. Sally started to cry, then she turned to run.

"Go ahead, run you killer bitch! But you'll never see Jimmy again if you do." Sally stopped dead in her tracks again, then turned back towards David,

"What have you done with my little boy?" She screamed. David was grinning from ear to ear. He had finally gotten her full attention.

"Well, my little killer bitch, I have him tucked away, safe and sound. As long as you do what I tell you to, he will be safe." David knew that he was in full control now. Sally was crying uncontrollably.

"What the hell do you want from me? And how do you know so much?" She was breaking down now, physically and emotionally. "I'll do whatever you want—just don't hurt Jimmy."

"I don't want to do anything to you, my dear. I just want your soul."

"What the hell are you talking about? Are you the fucking devil or something?" She was going out of her mind.

"Oh goodness no, sweetheart," David said laughing, "That's much too big of a job for me to handle. I'm just the guy who has a deal with 'Mr. Big' and I have to fulfill that deal soon— very soon."

"You're out of your mind if you think that I believe you!"

"Let me explain it to you, so that you can understand it, the way I explained it to Joe and his buddies. You see, they already took my deal."

Sally was getting sick to her stomach, her head was spinning, all she could think about was Jimmy. *Save Jimmy.*

"Now, here's the facts, honey. You're already dead."

"You're one crazy asshole!" Sally screamed, then turned and started to walk away. David snapped, grabbed her forearm,

squeezed hard, and spun her around, like a top. White pain
shot through her whole body! His face became deformed, his
teeth elongated, his eye's glowed red, and some dark green
substance, trickled out of his ear's and nose. It terrified her.

"Now listen closely, bitch," he growled, "you died in a train
crash back in Pennsylvania, not here. You, your son, and everyone else on that goddamned train are dead. You just don't
realize it yet because you were sleeping when it happened!
GET IT…SLEEPING!"

David lifted her two feet off the ground and was shaking
her with both hands. Her body was flopping around like a
rag doll.

"Do you understand me! DEAD! And you're already going
to hell for MURDER! The murder of your husband! So, just
make a deal with me for your soul, and I'll make sure Jimmy
doesn't find out about anything. He will be free to go to heaven.
I'll even get Dan to take him. You wouldn't want Jimmy to
know the truth, would you Sally?"

Sally couldn't comprehend any of this, but she knew one
thing: she did kill her husband, even if it was in self-defense.

"Come on Sally, time to make a deal. It'll be alright." David
said with compassion in his voice now.

"Are you sure Jimmy will be alright?" She asked
in desperation.

"Absolutely Sally. I give you my word." David knew he had
her now. Just a few more souls to go, and his deal with the
devil would be fulfilled.

"Okay, I'll do it. Just keep Jimmy away from all of this. Do
I sign something or what?"

"Oh no dear, just a hand shake is all that it takes." David
smiled as Sally held out her trembling hand. With tears rolling down her soft cheeks, she shook hands with David, and
whispered to herself, *please forgive me God.*

"Okay, now what about Jimmy?"

"He's being released as we speak, I promise." And with that statement, a rusted trunk lid from a old '36 Ford coupe popped open, much to Jimmy's surprise, setting him free.

CHAPTER 8

THE SEARCH

Dan woke up to the sound of birds singing their morning songs to each other. He swung his legs off the mildew mattress, walked over to the window and raised the dusty shade. He looked out to a gray, overcast morning. It looked like rain was coming soon. He didn't remember laying down, or how he even got in this room, but it sure felt good getting some sleep. He figured he must be in one of the guest rooms, just off of the main lobby.

He peeked out the window again. It was starting to rain. He noticed a lone, leafless tree about two hundred feet away. It was creating a silhouette against the smokey gray clouds. The old fashioned metal window blinds had a thick layer of dust clinging on them. Dan ran his index finger over one of them, shook his head and thought, *mom would never let this happen.* He started thinking about his mom, and then caught himself day dreaming.

"Dan!" A loud knock hit the door, "Dan! You gotta get up! We found Jimmy! But now Sally's missing!"

"Is that you Jerry?"

"Yeah, Dan, it's me, now come on, you gotta hurry!"

Jerry's voice faded as he ran outside and waited for Dan. Dan put on his socks and shoes, and headed for the door. Just then Jimmy pushed the door open and ran into Dan's arms.

"Dan! Dan! David hit me and then locked me in a dirty, old trunk of a car!" Jimmy started to cry now. "I heard you calling my name but I couldn't yell out, cause he put tape over my mouth and tied me up! And now my mom is missing, and we gotta go find her! Okay Dan?

"Okay Jimmy, slow down a little bit. How do you know David has your mom?"

"Because he's missing too," Jerry chimed in, sticking his head through the door opening, "we saw her go looking for Jimmy with him. We tried to stop her, but he convinced her that he knew where Jimmy was."

"Then why didn't you follow her?"

"Because you collapsed, and we brought you in here to get some sleep. Then Patti suggested we all get some rest before more people drop over or wander off in the dark and get lost. So that's what we did, and here we are."

"Well, that explains a lot." Dan said. "Let's go find Sally."

They all headed out the door. Hank was waiting for him outside. Dan stopped and shook his hand.

"Good to see you buddy. Would you and Bernie stay here and tend the wounded? Also, Sally might wander back here and need some help."

Hank didn't like the idea of staying behind, but Bernie had a look on her face.

"I guess so, Dan, but I would prefer being where the action is." Dan shook Hank's hand again, and told him how much he appreciated him doing this favor.

Outside now, Dan divided everyone into three groups. Patti, Jerry, and Jimmy were in Dan's group. "Okay, are we ready to go?" He asked.

"I think so," Patti replied, adjusting her backpack, "I just don't know which way to go."

"And I spotted four people coming down the trail five minutes ago when I was looking around." Jerry stated.

"Probably those FBI guys. Real wacko's. Alright, let's head for the trail you last saw Sally on."

Everybody agreed and followed Dan. They made their way up and down the narrow trail for a good hour, then they came to a fork. They stopped to take a break. Dan looked around and squatted down looking for foot prints. Nothing.

"Which way Dan?" Patti asked.

"I'm not sure. I'm not a very good tracker. In fact, I don't have a clue of what I'm looking for. I'll tell you what, you guys go to the left and I'll stay to the right. Okay?"

Jerry wasn't keen on the idea of splitting up, and Jimmy did not want to leave Dan for any reason.

"I don't know Dan, we really don't want to split up." Patti stated.

"I don't like the idea either, but I can't see another way around it, can you?" Jerry and Patti were thinking it over. Jimmy ran over to Dan, wrapped his arms around him a stated, "I'm going with you Dan, and I'm not letting you go until you say it's alright."

"Okay pal, you can go with me." Dan said laughing and hugged Jimmy real hard. "Jerry, you and Patti be careful, give a shout out if you see or hear anything, and we'll do the same. The pathways seam to go in the same general direction, maybe they hook back up together, farther up the trail. So every half hour or so, give a shout, OK?"

"You got it Dan. Are you sure you are feeling alright? You know, after last night and all?"

"Yes I'm fine Jerry. A good night sleep works wonders for an old guy like me. I'll see you two soon. Jimmy, let's move out."

"You got it Dan!" Jimmy replied, smiling up at Dan and then took his little hand and slipped into Dan's hand. "Dan, do you think my mom is safe? I'm really scared for her."

"I'm sure she's fine pal. We just have to find her and everything will be back to normal." Dan reassured Jimmy, but deep down, he knew she was in trouble. Dan and Jimmy walked carefully down the trail. The scent of the pine trees was invigorating. The chirping of the birds gave a positive spin on their journey. Dan was getting optimistic that they would find Sally and get her away from David. Every few minutes he or Jimmy would give a shout out for Sally and, once in a while, a shout out for Jerry and Patti. Jimmy started to slow down and tears we forming in his eyes.

"Dan…where's my mom?" He looked up at Dan. Tears started running down his rosy, red cheeks, Dan's heart was breaking. Jimmy could hardly talk. He was choking, trying to catch his breath. "Dan, I, I…I want my mom…where is she?" Dan dropped down on one knee and held his arms open.

"Come here big guy." Jimmy ran into his arms, he picked him up and gave him a giant hug, "Don't worry, pal. We're going to find your mother, I promise you. And I never go back on my word, so hang in there buddy, okay?"

"You promise, Dan?"

"Yes Jimmy, I promise."

"…Dan, my feet are hurting."

"No problem pal," Dan said, reaching under Jimmy's arms and swung him onto his broad shoulders. "How's that pal, now your taller then me! How's the view up there?" Jimmy laughed and wiped the tears off his face, with his shirt sleeve.

"Hey, I am really tall now, Dan! I can see everything! I can see for a hundred miles."

"That's great Jimmy! Keep a look out for your mom. I'm sure she's close." They continued walking for another half hour. Dan's shoulders were killing him by now, but he kept it to himself. They continued on, like two determined soldiers in search of their base camp.

———————

"Hank, somebody's out there." Bernie warned. Hank jumped up out of his musty chair.

"Who is it? Do you recognize them?" Bernie was peeking out of the dusty, old Venetian blinds. Hank came to her side to take a look.

"Looks like there's four of them—two of them look FBI, might be the one's Dan was talking about. But where's Hellen and Eli?"

Bernie didn't reply. They watched them closely as they began setting up their equipment.

"What are they doing, Hank? And what's all that fancy equipment for?"

"Beats me, Bernie, but let's wait and see what happens before we go out there to meet with them. Hell, maybe they don't even know that we're in here."

———————

"Harris, how do you know that they're in there?"

"I don't Pierce. Just a hunch, I guess. Stu, set that up over here, okay?"

They were almost ready now.

"Abe, you got the audio working yet?"

"Yes, we're all set to roll Ted." Abe said as he made some final adjustments.

"Hello! In the motel!" Harris shouted out. "You are not in any trouble what-so-ever. Repeat, you're not in any trouble."

Pierce rolled her eyes, thinking, that sounded so corny, like an old movie.

"My name is Agent Harris. I'm with the FBI. These are all my colleagues and we're here to help you."

"Help us what?" Hank shouted out, "and where's Eli and Hellen?"

Abe repeated what Hank asked to Harris, then handed him a set of headphones, so he could communicate for himself.

"Eli and Hellen are safe and sound," Harris said. "If you would all come out, I could explain everything to you."

"Can't come out, we've got wounded in here, and some are pretty bad."

"Would it be alright if we came in, then?"

"I don't know...let me talk it over with everybody and I'll let you know."

Hank turned to Bernie and asked, "Well, what do you think? Should we let them in?"

"I'm not sure Hank, I'm a little scared. And besides that, do you think they could stand all the excitement?" They turned and looked at the wounded, then walked over to them.

"What do you think, folks? Are you up for some company?"

They were all pretty weary, but most nodded their heads and smiled. Everyone agreed. Hank returned to the window, opened it up, and hollered out.

"Come on in, doors opened."

Harris grew a large smile on his tired face.

"You heard him guys. Let's grab the gear and go in for a visit." After setting up all of the equipment and getting comfortable, Harris explained the whole story to all of them, then took questions.

"So...what you're telling us...is that we are already dead."

"I'm afraid so ma'am," Harris answered in a somber voice.

"Well, if we're dead already, why do we hurt from our wounds?"

"You really don't, Ma'am. You think you feel pain, you think you're hungry, and so on, but your minds are playing tricks on you. It's like being in shock right after a car accident. Your subconscious mind takes over because you can't handle what just happened. In this case, while you were asleep, the train crashed in Pennsylvania, and your subconscious took over to protect you. You ended up out here, at crash site number two, thinking you were alive, but…"

Hank was having a hard time believing this whole thing. Bernie had a sweet smile on her face. She reached over and grasped Hank's hand.

"Hank," Bernie whispered, "we have been blessed, think about it. You and I would have never met if it weren't for this. And all the others too—Sally, Dan, Jimmy, all of them. Think about it Hank. It's all good."

She continued holding his hand, then it hit him, like a ton of bricks.

"You're right, Bernie. You're absolutely right. But what about Dan and the others? Somebody has to go and tell them. Get them back here so they can hear this from Agent Harris and be released."

Hank walked over to the wounded people, who were sitting in chairs and on the floor with old blankets wrapped around them and wearing meager smiles on their faces. They were looking up at him for answers.

"Here's the story everyone, as far as I can understand it." Hank looked at them with love in his heart, "Bernie and I believe that Agent Harris is right about everything, so stay calm and follow Agent Harris's instructions." This came as a shock to some of them, and a relief to others. Some were happy and some had tears in their eyes. Hank looked at Bernie and smiled.

"I can't stay here Bernie. I have to find the others, but I'll be back as soon as I can. I'll see you soon, one way or another."

With that said, Hank gave her a big hug goodbye, kissed her on the cheek and walked out the door.

"What do we do now Agent Harris?" Bernie asked. Everyone looked up at Harris.

"Just take it all in. Think about it, and then…just let go…"

The room was silent for a few moments until, suddenly, the roof disintegrated into a million fragments. The dusty old room began to shine with a brilliant light. Bernie walked over and joined the group. They all stood up together. Some held hands, and some hugged each other. Bernie was crying and smiling. Some of the people swore that they could hear the voice of God calling them. One by one, they ascended up through the old motel into the steel blue sky. As Bernie rose up, she was wondering if she looked presentable enough for this journey… *The Journey of a Lifetime…*

Harris and the others started packing up their equipment. Pierce was shaking her head and pacing around in circles.

"I don't know how you figured this out Harris, but you got this case 100% right." She hated to admit it, but when someone's right, they're right.

"I just got lucky Pierce, that's all. Let's go home guys."

"What do you mean Ted? What about the others?" Abe asked, confused.

"Let's just forget the others. They will find their way. I think we've seen enough miracles to last us a lifetime, don't you, Pierce?" She nodded her head, without saying a word.

Stu was more than happy to get off this mountain and this case. Abe wanted to see more but went along with the rest. Besides that, he had to process all the footage they had. *What a TV show this would make*, he thought.

It took over five hours to get down the mountain. They

finally made it all the way back to the campsite. Only one lonely police officer was still on site. Everything seemed to be back to normal. The officer asked Harris a few more questions, but Harris told them that nothing much happened. It was a dead end.

"What did you tell him that for?" Pierce asked.

"Do you really think he would have believed any of it?" Harris grinned.

They got in their dusty rental car, and drove away.

———————————

Dan saw a glimmer to his left. He turned. It was Patti and Jerry.

"Hey guys, over here!" Dan yelled out, "Jimmy, I'm going to bring you down now, okay?" He slipped Jimmy off his shoulders and they both ran over to meet Patti and Jerry. "How are you guys doing?" Dan asked.

"Pretty good! You see anything yet?" Jerry asked.

"We thought we heard some voices a while back, but it turned out to be nothing, how bout you guys?"

"Nothing yet, but we sure could use a break and some water." Jerry said.

"And how about you, Jimmy? Want a snack and some water?" Patti asked with a big smile, as she reached out and rubbed the top of Jimmy's hair.

"Sure, I'm starving."

"You're always starving," Dan said, laughing. After they finished eating, Jerry and Jimmy played a quick game of tag.

"Well guys, everybody ready to move out?" Dan asked. "We need to find Sally before dark."

They were tired and sore, but really wanted to find Sally for Jimmy's sake. Down the grassy trail they went. The sun was full in the deep blue sky, keeping them comfortably warm.

The smell of wild honey-suckle was thick in the gentle breeze. Honey bees criss-crossed over the pathway, and you could see the pollen floating all around. It was absolutely beautiful. Under better circumstances, this would be a perfect day for a picnic, Dan thought. But the feeling he had in his gut told him this wasn't going to be anything like a picnic.

They walked for a steady hour. Nobody complaining, no talking or joking around, just looking. Crickets were singing accompanied by the occasional crow call. Every now and then somebody would holler out Sally's name. The path led to an open hay field, where golden hay lined both sides of the narrow pathway. Dan held his arms out from his sides and gently caressed the top of the hay as he walked. He tipped his head back and closed eyes. Then he started to hum a song,

All our times have come here,
But now they're gone,
Seasons don't fear the reaper
Nor do the wind, the rain or the rain
Come on baby
Don't fear the reaper
Baby take my hand

Suddenly, a large black crow swooped down and hit Dan square in the forehead, giving off a horrid squeal, as it drew blood. Three more were circling fifty feet ahead, waiting to make their kill. Fear shot through everyone. Jimmy screamed. Dan got that feeling again, and now he knew what it meant.

"THERE THEY ARE!" Patti screamed, pointing up the pathway. Dan looked past the crows, maybe a hundred yards in front of them. It looked like Dave Cummings, Sally and five or six other people, although it was hard to tell from here. Patti and Jerry looked at Dan. Jimmy screamed for Sally. The blood rolled into Dan's eyes, blurring his vision for a few seconds. His hands were shaking, his throat was dry, and he couldn't think straight. He thought he was prepared for this moment, but he wasn't. He started running towards them as fast as he could. He didn't know if he should yell or try to surprise them. Jerry and Patti caught up to Dan.

"Where's Jimmy?"

"Right behind us, Dan."

They all stopped for a second. Dan scooped Jimmy right up into his arms. Tears were streaming down the boy's cheeks.

"Jimmy, stay with me pal, stay with me." Dan's heart was pounding right through his chest. Sweat was pouring off his forehead mixing with his blood. It stung and burned as it rolled into his eyes. His head hurt badly. and worse then that, he was slowing down now. He wanted to fall down and curl up in the golden hay, and just rest. Just as he thought he could go no farther, he spotted Sally.

"STAY BACK JIMMY!" Sally screamed. "Dan, keep him BACK!"

She was hysterical, and that bastard, David Cummings, was standing right next to her with his chest puffed out, looking like he was King Kong. Dan recognized some of the other people standing next to David and Sally. Jerry and Patti stopped short of the group and waited for Dan and Jimmy to catch up

"STOP RIGHT THERE, DANNY BOY!" David commanded, holding up his hand. "The game is over, Danny Boy, and I won!" He was so full of himself now, and he looked insane. "Now here's the way that it's going down, Danny Boy, you mind your manners, and do I as I tell ya, and little Jimmy will remain safe, GOT IT?"

The wind picked up and storm clouds were rushing in. The crows circled like hawks, diving lower with each rotation.

"Got what, you fucking asshole!"

"Now that's no way to talk to me, Danny Boy, especially with little Jimmy in your arms." With that, David swung his hand over the ground. Lightning flashed and thunder cracked, then instantly a storm cellar door appeared out of the ground. It was old and tattered, with paint curling off of the ancient wood. Smoke started seeping up through the cracks in the wood. The rotten smell of sulfur immediately hit the air, gagging Jimmy. More lightning and thunder crashed around them as it began to pour rain. David flicked his hand upwards and the doors flew open, causing the rusted, metal hinges to screech with pain. He pointed at Jack Beckman.

"Alright Jack, you know what you've done, and you committed suicide because of it, didn't you!" David laughed as he made this statement, "and you know what happens to people who commit suicide, don't you Jackie Boy…"

"But you hired me to do it." Jack was going crazy. His head spinning. He held his hands on his head, trying to help hold his thoughts together. "YOU HIRED ME, REMEMBER?" He was crying like a baby now.

"Jackie, Jackie, Jackie, don't be such a pussy. You were a bad little boy and now you're gonna pay for it. Now march down those steps and we'll see you soon." David said, loving every second. He turned and looked Dan right in the eyes. "Watch this, Danny Boy…you're gonna *love* this part."

Jack turned and walked slowly towards the opening in the ground. When he reached the first step, he carefully stepped down, as though he was testing the water temperature of a spring lake. That's when David kicked him square in the back, sending him down the steps in an instant! Jack screamed half in surprise and half in pain. He landed on the bottom step, which was about eight feet below the ground. He stood up, face bloody and missing some teeth. David loved the whole scene, and started laughing his ass off once again. Just then, Jack got sucked into some kind of membrane surface. He was stuck on it, face first, arms and legs spread wide open. All you could hear was a loud mumbling as he was pulled through the membrane, slowly, until he was out of sight.

David was in a demonic state, chanting and howling, jumping up and down. That's when Joe Rodgers joined him. Jerry and Patti were in disbelief. Dan covered Jimmy's eyes. Sally was on her knees, praying. The storm intensified.

"Okay, Joey! You're next! Jump down there and kick some ass!" Without one bit of hesitation, Joe jumped down the steps and dove through the membrane. David clapped with approval. "Now that's a *man!*" David turned to Pete, "Pete Perry, come on down! It's your turn to play... *The Price for Your Sins."*

Pete looked scared, and not so eager to go, but he did make the deal. So he obliged David and down the steps he went. When he reached the bottom he peered into the abyss ad didn't like what he saw. It started to tug on him. He resisted, but it was too late. He screamed as he disappeared.

"Are you having fun yet, Danny Boy? Wait, it gets better. Stevie Boy! It's your turn now!"

Steve kept stuttering, "ba,ba,but I tried to help Joey, I really did." He walked down the stairs backwards, reaching out for David, "I tried, I tried...Please..." He reached the bottom step, still searching for forgiveness in David's eyes.

"Turn around Stevie Boy and walk in like a man." David's laughter echoed loudly. "MOVE, Steve!"

Slowly he went through the opening.

"Ahhhhh, Monica, my second favorite. You're next sweetie pie! Ready to go?" Monica threw him the finger, and walked down the steps with her head held high. Just before she walked into the membrane, she turned, and told David to get fucked.

"And Tom! Poor Tom—you were in the wrong place at the

wrong time, buddy! Not your fault—after all, you were just doing your civic duty, right pal? I almost feel bad sending you down, but…I do have to make my quota!"

Tom was crying, hanging his head low as he walked down the steps. He was shaking, not sure what was going to happen to him. He knew that he did nothing wrong but this guy made a deal with him, and that was that.

David slowly turned towards Sally with a big smile. Like a barker at a fair, he announced:

"AND NOW! Last but not least! My favorite, and yours too! Mrs. Sally Weeks!" David was loving it. He bowed down and gestured with his arm, pointing toward the steps. *It's your turn.*

"No Mommy! NO! Don't hurt my Mommy!"

"Easy Jimmy, we won't let anything happen to your mommy." Patti said.

"Come on David, let her go, would ya?" Dan was desperate, he wasn't sure how this was going to turn out. He would beg, if he had to.

"Danny boy, she's going of her own free will, aren't you my dear?" Sally slowly nodded her head in confirmation. Dan couldn't believe his eyes. What kind of a spell did David have on her? Sally stood up and walked over to the door, stepped onto the stone steps and moved downwards. Jimmy was screaming at the top of his lungs. At the last step, she turned around and took one last look at her dear Jimmy.

"I love you," she cried out, then felt the pull of the membrane as she stuck to it.

The the invisible force pulled her backwards. She reached her arms out at Jimmy and Dan, as tears rolled down her pale cheeks. Her terror was so strong, knowing she was entering Hell forever, that it distorted her facial features. Her leg muscles strained as she planted her feet on the stone floor, trying to resist the pull. She leaned forward, but her arms were stuck fast. She gave out one more scream.

Jimmy wanted to save her, and he begged Dan to let him go. Dan held on to Jimmy with all he had, and Jimmy fought Dan with all he had. Jerry and Patti were in shock. They didn't have a clue of what to do. David stood between them and Sally, grinning and laughing at the whole scene. He wasn't laughing because it was funny, however—he was laughing because he was finally fulfilling the pact that he made with the Devil.

"Damn their souls! I'm going to make it!" David yelled at the top of his lungs. Then he focused on little Jimmy. He squatted down, still watching Jimmy closely. Then he pointed at Sally.

"Jimmy! Go with your Mom! Look at her! She needs your help, NOW!"

"Shut your mouth David, or I'll…" Dan started,

"…or you'll what, Jensen? Come on Danny Boy, I'm right here! What are you waiting for? Let the kid go and we'll see what your made out of." He started his insane laughter again.

Dan's whole body ached. His temples were twisted into burning time bombs. That's when Jimmy landed a backward kick that landed square into Dan's groin. He doubled over in pain while Jimmy broke free and took off.

"NO JIMMY! Come back!" Dan looked up from his hunched position and Jimmy was almost in his mother's arms. Dave Cummings cheered with victory!

"That a boy, Jimmy! Now just tell me I can have your soul, and you and your mom can be together forever!"

"You can have it! Just let me be with my Mom!"

"DONE DEAL!" David was on a super high.

"NO Jimmy, NO! He's tricking you Jimmy! WAIT!"

It was too late. Jimmy was hugging his mom. Half of her body was through the membrane. She clung to Jimmy.

At this point, her mind was gone. She didn't even try to stop Jimmy.

"Go save him Danny Boy! You're the big hero, aren't you? Didn't you promise Sally that you would protect him?" Dan was in tears now. Jimmy was starting to go through the membrane.

"ALL RIGHT you bastard! You win! Just let me save Jimmy, I'll take his place!"

"Gotta say the magic words, Danny Boy! Better hurry, he's almost in."

"God forgive me! You can have my soul!" As quickly as he said it, Dan hit the membrane wall, and Jimmy was in Patti's arms.

Dan was sucked into the next membrane. It was much larger than the first, almost like a giant spider web. He was stuck to it face first. Through the webbing of the sticky membrane, he saw Sally stuck on the next one in front of his. He tried to yell to her, but she didn't respond. Web after web, each one getting harder and stronger, one would tear open and then another, shooting him to the next, each time knocking the breath out of him and bruising his ribs. He went through a total of seven webs or membranes. Then, he was finally in. The heat was unbearable, and the sulfur smell was horrible. He was gagging and holding onto his stomach, then he started to vomit. Sweat rolled off his forehead as he crunched into a fetal position.

He laid there for a few minutes, then he spotted Sally over in a corner, face down. He ran to her and rolled her over onto her back. He looked into her eyes. The blue was gone, replaced by dark grey. Crusted tears edged down her worn cheeks. She didn't blink, just stared at Dan, looking straight through him. She was hollow inside now, just a shell of a mother, with a faint memory of a little boy with blonde hair, blue eyes, and a big smile.

Dan held her in his arms, caressing her soiled hair, hating everything about this "*Ride of a lifetime.*" He couldn't understand where it all went wrong. What had he done to deserve all of this? What could he had done differently? All of these thoughts ran through his head. He bent down and whispered into Sally's ear.

"Sally, I'll get us out of here. I promise.

———————

David Cummings completed his side of the deal and was long gone by the time Dan was holding Sally in his arms.

Jerry and Patti held Jimmy's hands as they slowly walked down the pathway. The rain had stopped by now, little puddles dotted the path every now and then. Normally, Jimmy would be jumping in them and splashing everyone. Right now, he didn't even see them. He didn't see the butterflies, the birds, or even the sun shinning bright in the sky. Patti looked up and felt the warm rays of the sun hitting her. She eagerly took in the heat, giving her hope that they would find their way to a new home, where they could be safe and happy.

"Hey guys, hold up!"

They turned around to spot Hank a hundred feet behind them.

"Holy shit, it's Hank!" Patti yelled out. Jimmy didn't react. They waited for Hank to catch up.

"Hank!" Jerry shouted and instantly gave him a big hug. "You're a sight for sore eyes, Hank! Where's everybody else?"

"It's a long story…how bout you guys? Where's Dan and Sally?" That question made Jimmy start crying. Patti hugged him tightly.

"That's a long story too, Hank, and you're not going to believe it."

Jerry started to tell him everything that took place in

the past two hours. Hank listened on in disbelief, but after what he witnessed this morning, nothing shocked him now. After Jerry finished, everyone comforted Jimmy as best as they could. Hank waited a while before beginning to tell him his story. He described it very slowly so they could take it all in. Hank could tell that Jerry and Patti weren't quite grasping the whole situation.

"So you mean to tell us that we're already dead?" Patti exclaimed. "And we have been since when?"

"Since the first crash. Or, I should say, the real crash." It was hard for Hank to describe, and he hoped he was getting the facts straight.

"So, what's it all mean, Hank," Jerry asked with a strange look on his face. "Are we supposed to be in heaven?"

Hank knew he had to get this right. "I suppose it does. Ah…I could explain how Agent Harris said it happened. I mean, I didn't see it for myself, but this is how he explained it. When Hellen and Eli found out what happened, they smiled and started to rise up, you know, in the air. Then they just went up. Agent Pierce said it was a beautiful thing."

"Okay then. Just hold hands. That's it, everybody hold hands. Now just relax, look up and let's go home" Within a few short minutes, they all felt a beautiful sensation tingling through their bodies. Jimmy was smiling and laughing as his feet left the ground. Jerry and Patti were next, and then Hank.

CHAPTER 9

THE THIRD SEARCH PARTY

As they walked down the pathway, John decided to get to know Monica and Tom a little better. He would break the ice with Tom, then hopefully Monica.

"So Tom, where ya from?"

"I'm from a little town called Lost Oaks in West Virginia. It's a great place to live. You'd love it there. It's nestled in the hills—lot's of trees and fields, hot summers and warm winters. I sure do miss it."

"Sounds nice Tom. Tell me more about it"

"Well, it's a small town, population is under six hundred. But we have everything we need, ya know, like a post office, gas station, a nice diner with homemade pies for desert. And of course we've got our own court house, which also doubles as the sheriff's office... yeah, I sure do miss it."

"How 'bout you, Monica? Where you from?"

"The city." She answered short. *Not much of a talker*, John thought. You couldn't shut her up back at the camp. But now: pure ice. She looked different too. Her hair seemed darker, pitch black almost, and it was poker straight. Her eyes were dark green, with a speck of yellow. She looked aggravated.

"Yeah, me too—the Bronx. And you?"

"What is this, twenty questions, or something?"

"No, I'm just making small talk to pass the time. That's all, no big deal."

"Well, what's your story, since you're so hell bent on getting to know me?"

"My story is pretty simple. I got married right after school, which only lasted three years. Had a few part time jobs, got heavy into golf for a while, turned pro five years ago. I was headed out to the coast, thought I'd take the scenic root, and ended up here, wherever here is."

"That sounds real nice John," Tom said, "Ya still play the game?"

"Sounds like a dull life, if you ask me. No wonder your wife left you." Monica added, with a laugh.

"I left her, just to set the record straight. So how 'bout you Monica? How's your life exciting, compared to ours?"

"Bet your ass it is." She was getting pissed at this little game that John was playing, so she figured that she would set him straight, right here and right now.

"To start off with, I'm 5-foot-2, 113 pounds. and I'll bet that I can kick the shit out of you in any gym. I can outrun you, outsmart you, and outthink you. You name it, candy-ass, and I'll beat you." John was caught totally off guard with that statement.

"Secondly, I run two successful businesses that I built on my own. I was married for eight months, and I threw the bastard out after he slapped me. I spit in his face, and he is paying dearly for that slap, five years dearly." She laughed out loud on that statement.

"And if I tell Tom over there that it's raining right now,

he'll believe it, *or I'll make him believe it.* Get my drift, John? So shove this game up your ass."

"Hey, look guys," Tom broke in, "Is that a cabin or something, up ahead?"

Tom was very excited about his find. He started to run towards the structure, mostly to get away from Monic's rant and partially hoping to find help. When John and Monica reached the cabin, Tom was already inside.

"What do ya see, Tom?" Monica yelled out.

"Not much," he responded in a disappointed voice, "Just some old, dusty furnishings and empty cupboards." Then he walked out of the cabin without saying another word and he noticed Monica had a disappointed look on her face.

"Well, let's keep going. It's getting late and we have to turn around and go back in a half-hour." John stated.

"Turn around a go back? Are you friggin' kidding me?" Monica shouted, "We're just getting started! We've got to find help!"

"Whoa! Take it easy Monica, what's your problem?"

"I'll tell you what's my problem! You're not my boss and I'm sure Tom feels the same way! Further more, we've got to find food and help to get out of this fucked up situation! Understand?" John was totally shocked. He didn't know what to say or do, but he had to think of something fast.

"Hold on now," Tom stuttered, "Let's not fight with each other. Let's try to work this out, okay?" That made sense to John, but Monica was on a warpath.

"There's nothing to work out Tom! You see, John here's got himself a girlfriend back at camp that he wants to get back to—you promised her, didn't ya, Johnny Boy? He doesn't give a shit about us, or everyone else. Only himself!"

"That's bullshit Monica! You don't know what you're talking about."

"Is it?" Monica smiled, then turned back towards Tom. "You know what Tom, I think he's lying, and I think we should go search for help and let this asshole go back to his girlfriend. What do you say Tom? Do you want to go with me, or with that loser?"

Tom didn't say a word and he didn't look John in the eye. He just turned and walked away with Monica. John shook his head in disbelief as he watched them stroll down the path, chatting with each other like best friends.

After a few lonesome minutes, John headed back to the camp, not knowing how he was going to explain all of this to everybody. As he walked along, he began to hear nature's music flow into his ears—bee's buzzing and crickets chirping. And then, a gun shot.

Instantly causing a faint wisp of air from a bullet that blew right by his left temple, it made his brown wavy hair fluff up as it creased his scalp. The next sound he heard was another gun shot. This time it didn't miss. John felt the ground meet him in what felt like slow motion. He fell face first into the sweetest smelling grass he'd ever smelled. That second bullet caught him in the middle of his shoulder blades.

Things were going black fast. He struggled hard to keep his wits. He couldn't move. That last bullet must have hit his spinal column. He wanted so much to see Hellen one last time, to say goodbye to her. As he lay on the ground, taking in the sweet aromas of Mother Earth, he had a warm feeling reassuring him not to worry.

The last sound he ever heard was some evil giggling behind him in the woods.

Monica and Tom continued their journey down the pathway as though they were college sweethearts. Laughing and joking, not a care in the world, until…

"Monica! Tell me your life story honey." David Cummings shouted, "and tell me who's your new friend?" Ice cold chills ran down Monica's spine. She never thought in a million years that she would ever hear that voice again. She had doubled crossed David years ago in a rip-off scam. And now, here he was.

"David! How are you doing? Never thought I would see you again! And now here you are, out in the middle of nowhere." She was afraid to look up at him. Tom was speechless, as he looked at them both. Monica started to sweat and felt like she was going to pass out.

"Monica, Monica, Monica. Dear sweet Monica." He smiled, shaking his head. He reached out to shake Tom's hand, "and who might you be, stranger?"

Tom felt instant cold run up his arm as he shook David's large, intimidating hand. His mouth was dry and he could barely get out the words.

"Ta, ta, Tom, Fra Franklin…sir… nice to meet ya…"

"Well, it's a pleasure to meet you, too, Tom. My name is David Cummings. Looks like you've got yourself a pretty nice girlfriend there, Tommy—it's okay if I call you Tommy, isn't it, my boy?"

"Sure thing, sir. Call me me whatever you like."

"That's nice of you to say Tommy. And listen, don't be so formal! Just call me 'David.' After all, we're gonna be close friends, right?" Tom gulped and nodded his head as he tried to remove his hand from David's. He knew David could shatter his hand with one little squeeze.

David turned his attention back to Monica. He looked her over, and a grin grew on his face. "My dearest Monica. I've missed you so! Oh, the memories we shared. Remember dear, when we shared a bed, many moons ago?"

"Please David, I didn't mean to…"

"…'to' what, my dear? Turn me over to the cops? Have them interrogate me, beat a confession out of me, then throw me in prison for the rest of my life? To have me rot away in that stinking hell? Getting the shit kicked out of me every goddamned night, 'till I had to make a deal with the *fucking devil* just to keep my sanity!" David roared. He was building himself up into a frenzy.

"What do you have to say for yourself, bitch!?" He was there now in full force! Just like with Joey, he was raging. His eyes were bulging, and he started ascending off the ground.

"Now it's *my* turn to make a deal!" he screamed. Tom couldn't breath. He fell to the ground, landing on his knees, not taking his eyes off of David. Monica was terrified, tears rolling down her face. She tried to run away, but she was frozen to the ground.

"Please David… I'm sorry!" She begged.

He screamed "Get over here NOW, bitch!"

She dropped to her knees, and started to pray, but she knew it was useless. He owned her—mind, body and soul. David slowly walked over to her, and placed his hand on the top of her head. She was shaking uncontrollably…

"We made a deal, my dear—remember?" She nodded her head in agreement, "and now I'm collecting on that deal. Say it, bitch." He demanded.

"Yes David…it's a deal…."

"Done deal! Done fucking DEAL!" He'd won again.

Tom looked on in horror. He didn't have a clue of what was taking place. Then David turned to him.

"Wanna make a deal, Tommy Boy? You can go and live with your girlfriend Monica, if you take my deal." Tom looked at Monica, she was shaking her head 'no.' She looked so scared, kneeling there, crying her eyes out. She needed him, he just knew it. He had to help her.

"OK, I'll do it." Tom yelled out!

David loved it. It was too easy. He shook hands with Tom and said, "Welcome to the club, Tommy Boy! Now let's dance, mother fuckers!"

After the all-night party ended, David took Monica and Tom to join the others. They all met in a beautiful hayfield. It looked like heaven on earth. The hay was swaying gently in the warm breeze, the sun was shining down, turning everything in sight to a golden brown, the birds were singing in the apple trees. Tom thought that last night might have been a bad dream. Just a bad dream. And today, in this beautiful place, everything was going to be all right. Maybe he and Monica would become closer or even a couple. He was sure that she had a good side.

47717844R00113

Made in the USA
Middletown, DE
10 June 2019